THE GOODSPEED
TOKEN

To
Michael
with love
Thanks for all you
created

BY
JON DAY

ISBN-10: 1483930769
ISBN-13: 9781483930763

Library of Congress Control Number: 2013905986
CreateSpace Independent Publishing Platform
North Charleston, SC

FOR

JULIA AND SOPHIA

CHAPTER 1

"Where is he?" Lilly Kemp asked.

She skated back and forth impatiently on her Rollerblades in front of the snow leopard's cage at the Central Park Zoo in New York City. It wasn't a cage with bars. A wire net separated the wild animal from the humans, and inside was a scene from nature with tall grasses, trees, and rocks. As nice as any cage could be, Lilly thought, although there were too many places where the leopard could keep out of sight when he wasn't feeling sociable, like now.

"He can't hide all day," Lilly said to her younger brother Sebastian. She held her inexpensive camera ready to shoot the instant the leopard appeared.

"I really need a picture of him for my project."
Exhibition day for the middle school science fair was
rapidly approaching.

"That'll be difficult," Sebastian said.

"I already know that. We've been here an hour and
he hasn't come out of hiding once."

"That's because he's sleeping."

Lilly knew Sebastian was about to make up one of
his stories. She usually played along, pretending to
believe, but today her temper was a little short because
she had not gotten the photographs she needed. "You
know this for a fact?" Lilly challenged.

Sebastian was not discouraged. "Absolutely."

Lilly stared into the cage, wishing the leopard
would come into view. Sebastian circled his sister
slowly on his Razor scooter.

"You see," he began, "last night after you went to
sleep, I climbed out our bedroom window and came
here to the zoo. It's so peaceful at night. The snow
leopard told me that if I let him out, he would give
me a ride. I opened the cage door and climbed onto
his back. He said to hold on tight, and it was a good
thing I did because he went from standing still to full
speed in one stride. He ran so fast my eyes watered
from the wind. We sped into Times Square, and all
the cars and taxis were jammed up, blocking our
way. So he leaped up and ran on top of the cars. You

should have seen the surprise on the tourists' faces as we flew by.

"We galloped over the water all the way to the Statue of Liberty and never sank. He climbed up the outside, and we sat on the statue's head to rest a while. Then we ran home past Dad's old office building and past school, and the leopard brought me to our building and went back to the zoo."

Sebastian yawned as if he too were exhausted from his adventure. "So you can see why he would be tired and need a nap."

"Get real, Sebastian," Lilly said.

It was almost five o'clock, and the zoo was closing. Lilly called her mother on her cell phone to tell her that she and her brother were heading home. She pulled on her helmet and her backpack, tightening the straps securely so the pack fit snugly against her. Sebastian took hold of a strong rope attached to Lilly's backpack. He hooked the loop at one end around his scooter's handlebars. He put on his baseball batting helmet with a large 2 on the back and a chess piece, a knight, glued to the top.

"Ready for blastoff," he said.

Lilly was tall for her age, and she was strong. Sebastian was short, the smallest boy in the sixth grade at Amsterdam Prep, so he was not too heavy a load for Lilly. She Rollerbladed out of the zoo, pulling her brother behind her into Central Park.

To a visitor the park could be a maze of roads, walking paths, playing fields, wooded areas, and ponds, but Lilly never got lost here. It was her backyard.

When she was younger, she climbed on the jungle gyms and swung high on the swings in the Diana Ross Playground near the 81st Street and Central Park West entrance. She played in a soccer league on the North Meadow fields. She rowed with her family on the boat pond. Before her father left, she Rollerbladed beside him when he jogged in the park, and he taught her how to navigate by using familiar landmarks—like the sculpture of the famous sled dog Balto—and even the position of the sun at certain times of day.

With her mother and Sebastian, Lilly had gone on what her science teacher mom called "park voyages" to study local plants, trees, and animals.

Today Lilly pulled her brother by the Chess and Checkers House near the Wollman ice skating rink. Outside the eight-sided, roundish building, a white-haired man played chess against a young Hispanic dude with a Mohawk haircut and tattoos.

"Hi, Mr. B!" Sebastian yelled, and the old man waved.

Lilly skated to their apartment building, which was not far from the Museum of Natural History in Manhattan's West Side neighborhood.

In their lobby Lilly opened the mailbox for apartment 1A with a key. On his tiptoes Sebastian eagerly peered inside. Empty.

In a squeaky voice, Sebastian said, "Nothing for you today, Sebastian. Maybe tomorrow," as if the mailbox were talking to him. He looked a little sad.

But he smiled when he saw a plastic bag hanging from the doorknob to his apartment. Inside was a plastic board with many different electronic pieces attached to it.

"Cool," he said. "A motherboard."

Sebastian was building a computer from parts he found in discarded computers that residents put in the basement trash room. Mitch, the TV actor who lived in 1C and wore big hats, knew about Sebastian's project, and he sometimes supplied used parts.

Lilly put her apartment door key into the lock and immediately heard Miss Flannigan's voice from behind the closed door across the lobby. "Go away!" Miss Flannigan said. "I'm dialing nine-one-one!"

Even the slightest noise in the lobby caused Miss Flannigan to threaten to phone the police. Before Lilly and Sebastian were born, her apartment had been robbed, and she was certain the robbers would come back to steal what they didn't get the first time. She had four locks on her door. Mitch nicknamed her Miss Fear-again.

"It's just Lilly and Sebastian coming home from school, Miss Flannigan," Lilly said with a smiley voice.

When they entered the small apartment, their mother, Jean, was preparing dinner in the kitchen. The room next to the kitchen had only enough space for a table where the children ate their meals and often did homework, and for an old TV with two armchairs that used to be comfortable. Jean had one bedroom. Lilly and Sebastian shared the other.

Lilly stored her Rollerblades in a closet next to Sebastian's scooter and went into the kitchen to help. As she washed lettuce for a green salad, she told her mother that she hadn't gotten a close-up photo of the darned snow leopard. Jean suggested Lilly find pictures on the Internet, but Lilly knew that wouldn't work. She wanted a good color photograph, and recently their printer broke. Sebastian was only able to fix it so it printed in black-and-white.

Sebastian set the table with placemats, forks, and spoons as he played chess against a computer program he named Warner, after his chess rival at school.

The screen flickered and went dark. "Oh man," he said to himself. "What a piece of junk."

Sebastian gently tapped the side of the old laptop several times, and the screen came back to life.

He concentrated on the game and didn't even look up when a gray squirrel with a bandage around one leg jumped on the table and then perched on his shoulder.

A month ago Lilly rescued the nearly dead squirrel, which had been attacked by a dog. She brought the unconscious animal home, where she carefully cleaned the dog bite on the squirrel's leg and wrapped it in a bandage.

When it regained consciousness, the squirrel was terrified and raced around the apartment, scampering into Jean's bedroom. She slammed the door shut, and they heard jars and bottles crash to the floor as the panicked animal ran atop shelves and a bureau trying to escape. Jean was just about to call the police when Sebastian cracked the door opened.

"Hello, squirrel," he said in a calm voice. "I'm your friend."

"Don't go in there, Seb," his mother warned.

"It's OK, Mom. He told me he won't hurt us."

Sebastian pulled a bag of dried cranberries, his favorite snack, out of his pants pocket and stepped into the room. In just a moment, the ruckus stopped. Lilly and Jean poked their heads in. Surrounded by his mother's hairbrush, jars of lotion, and a broken picture frame the terrified animal had knocked off a bureau,

Sebastian sat on the floor with the squirrel perched on his shoulder. The animal munched contentedly on a cranberry.

"Sebastian… how did you do that?" Jean asked.

"Do what, Mom?"

"Get the squirrel to stop running crazy wild around the room."

"He was just frightened and told me that a snack would calm him down."

Lilly knew her brother made friends with animals easier than he did with people. He could approach and pet any cat or dog he met on the street, even the vicious-looking pit bulls. But that was the first time he made friends with a wild animal.

He named the squirrel Checkmate, which is the move in chess when you defeat your opponent. He trained it to not go to the bathroom in the apartment and to stop hiding acorns in the chair cushions by the TV. He had tamed the squirrel so it was as friendly as a puppy.

And Sebastian talked to it like it understood human speech. Now he asked, "What do you think, Checkmate? Do I move my knight or my bishop?"

In a higher voice, as if the squirrel were actually advising him, he answered, "Move the bishop to take the pawn."

Sometimes the idea that her child was carrying on a conversation with a little furry animal worried Sebastian's mother.

She dished out pasta with vegetables for her family and made an extra plate. "Please take this over to Mr. B, Sebastian," she said.

☆ 14

CORK BOARD

CHAPTER 2

M r. Bernstein lived next to Miss Flannigan across the lobby.

He and Mrs. Bernstein had been married sixty-three years, and after she died during the winter, he sometimes forgot to eat. Sebastian knocked three times and entered. In a city where everyone locked their doors all the time, Mr. B did not. He once told Sebastian that he believed most people were good, and locks could not keep out the ones who weren't.

Mr. B sat in his big chair surrounded by newspapers. Every day he read three newspapers, each in a different language.

"Hi, Mr. B. Pasta again. Sorry."

"Delightful," Mr. Bernstein said. "Will I see you tomorrow at the Chess and Checkers House? I've just read about a chess match in Russia, and the winner used a wonderful plan I want to show you."

Sebastian promised he would be there.

"And keep a sharp eye out when you come. Somehow a coyote found its way to the park," Mr. Bernstein warned as he pointed to a blurry picture in one of his newspapers. It was not entirely clear if the animal was a wild coyote or just a thin, runaway dog.

At dinner Sebastian spun a story about a coyote that came to New York City because it really hated the wilderness.

When he was seven years old, Sebastian became so sick that he had to stay in bed in a darkened room for almost a year. To fight the boredom, he entertained Lilly, the nurses, and doctors who cared for him with stories. Sometimes his tales were about actual events at school or in the park or from TV, but he often added imagined details so they would be funnier or scarier. Some stories were entirely made up, and these often were based on his wishes and dreams and fears. Jean called all these creations "Sebastian-ations."

The coyote hated the nights in the wilderness, Sebastian began. Noises from the dark terrified him, like the ones that spooked Sebastian when he spent that awful week at the YMCA camp in the Pine Barrens of southern New Jersey. And, since squirrels and chipmunks were too cute to harm, the coyote had to eat birds.

Sebastian played the role of the sophisticated coyote, speaking in a slow, dignified voice that sounded like Upper School English teacher Dr. Posen, who pronounced almost every syllable.

"Birds! Do you have any idea how dis-gus-ting bird feathers taste?" Sebastian the coyote said. "Worse, they stick in your fangs. What I really like is brick-oven pizza and Chinese food, par-tic-u-lar-ly General Tso's chicken cooked Hunan style. I enjoy visiting the Museum of Natural His-tor-y because it's all about us an-i-mals. The subways are ex-cel-lent transportation, but my favorite way to get around town is in taxi cabs, so I can stick my head out the back window and feel the bre-eze in my face."

Sebastian told them about where the coyote liked to shop for the latest style in dog collars and where the best salon was to get a decent fur-cut. By the time they finished their meal, both his mother and sister were laughing out loud about the big-city coyote.

After dinner Jean, Lilly, and Sebastian washed the dishes in the cramped kitchen, and then it was Sebastian's turn to take the trash down to the cans in the building's basement. Besides the garbage and recycling, there was a shopping bag filled with clothes and a pair of large red sneakers.

Each month her husband was away, Jean threw out more of his clothes. When his mother wasn't looking, Sebastian snuck them into the apartment and stashed them in the back of his closet. Like tonight.

His and Lilly's bedroom wasn't much bigger than the closet. When they lived in a larger apartment upstairs on the sixth floor, each child had their own room. That was before their father left for California. After that Jean had to move her family to this smaller first-floor apartment with its cheaper rent.

The kids' bedroom had just enough space for a bunk bed and two small Ikea desks side by side. A confusion of computer parts that looked to Lilly as if Sebastian had dumped them there from a trash can littered his desk.

One computer part had wandered onto Lilly's tidy, well-organized desk, and she tossed it back into what he called "the genius junk heap."

"Do you mind?" she asked sarcastically.

Sebastian often did not answer his sister when she used that tone of voice.

A large corkboard was attached to the wall above the desks. On Sebastian's side were many ribbons he won at chess tournaments, a large poster of Yankee shortstop Derek Jeter, and a photo of the family taken in front of the huge, ancient Colosseum arena in Rome, Italy. Sebastian sat on his father's shoulders waving a play sword. VENI. VIDI. VICI. was written on the photo.

On her side of the corkboard, Lilly tacked a calendar marked with upcoming school events and some photos. One was of her when she was younger, climbing a rock while her father stood below, ready to catch her if she fell. Another photo showed her reading a fat book as she lay on the floor of a sun-drenched living room, her head resting on the stomach of a large white dog. In another picture she used a doctor's stethoscope as she pretended to examine Sebastian, who was in a hospital bed looking very small and frail.

Lilly climbed to her top bunk to read about snow leopards. Sebastian screwed the computer part Mitch had left him into a metal computer case. He tried to attach its wires to another part, but the connectors were a different size and would not plug in.

Frustrated, he went to the window and sat on the wide ledge, looking out. Checkmate jumped up onto his lap. Sebastian heard footsteps and became excited as they got closer. A tall man strode by and kept going down the block. Sebastian sat back against the window frame. His shoulders sagged with disappointment.

"Dad's coming home," Sebastian said. "He just has to finish building the biggest, most powerful computer in the universe."

Lilly looked at Sebastian with sadness in her eyes. "Will it be more powerful than the one you're building?"

"Of course. The one he's making is going to be smarter than you. Smarter than me. Smarter than Einstein, even. It will be so smart that it can figure out how to solve any problem in the world. No more bullies. No more starving children. Everyone will be big and strong."

"How about divorce?" Lilly asked. "What can the computer do about that?"

"As easy to find a solution as one plus one equals three."

That made Lilly smile.

Sebastian petted Checkmate. "Figuring all this out takes time, but once Dad's finished, he'll come up our street and walk right through the front door."

"Wake up to the facts, Seb," Lilly whispered to herself. "You're dreaming."

CHAPTER 3

Lilly, Sebastian, and Jean walked from their apartment building to Amsterdam Prep every day, unless it was raining really hard or a winter ice storm made the sidewalks dangerously slippery.

Some of the other students arrived on foot with one or more of their parents. Many kids came by taxicab or car. Some arrived in big, black, very shiny sport utility vehicles or limousines that Jean called "movie-star cars." Monica Green got out of one of those and walked right by Lilly and her family without so much as a hello.

Monica was not shy in sharing her conviction that she was not only the prettiest but also the smartest girl in middle school, and the teachers surely should have understood that she was entitled to the Bates Prize. The teachers awarded the prize to the student who was best at math, and last year Lilly won. Like Lilly, Monica was an A+ student, and Monica's parents protested to the principal that the math teachers had been unfair, favoring Lilly because her mother was a fellow teacher at the school.

The principal encouraged the teachers to reconsider, partly because Monica's father was a rich and powerful real estate developer who donated a lot of money to the private school. But the teachers stuck to their decision, telling the principal that Lilly and Monica were in the same advanced math class and Lilly had done better on the tests and homework. Monica had not spoken to Lilly since. That did not bother Lilly. She thought Monica was a little too conceited.

At lunch Monica and her friends always sat at the table near the entrance to the cafeteria so they would be seen by everyone coming in or leaving. Sebastian often sat by himself, and today Lilly joined him. Their table was right next to Monica's.

Unlike Monica, who wanted to be the most popular girl in the middle school, Lilly had a small number of close friends. Most were, like her, members of the math and glee clubs. A few were from the coed soccer team she played on, like Josh Roberts, whom some girls thought was the best-looking boy in eighth grade.

Lilly could hear Monica boasting about the trip to Europe she was going to take with her mother during summer vacation. They would stay in the best hotels in the world and eat at five-star restaurants. Lilly didn't know what five-star restaurants were, but she figured they probably served the kind of expensive food that a conceited person could be conceited about.

Lilly was not interested in summer plans. She was very excited about her science fair project. She told her friends how the snow leopards lived in remote Asian mountains, where they were hunted and killed for their beautiful fur. The leopards would soon be extinct if people did not do more to protect them. At the next table, Monica stopped talking about herself long enough to listen to what Lilly planned for her project.

Sebastian finished his lunch, took his tray to the clean-up area, and then walked by a table in a corner of the cafeteria where a skinny boy played chess against himself while munching on the first of three cheeseburgers stacked beside him on a tray. This was Warner. Though he was only in Lilly's grade, he was the chess champion of all Amsterdam Prep, including the high school. Sometimes Sebastian heard the word "brilliant" when the teachers talked about Warner. Sebastian played chess against him once and lost badly.

He watched Warner move a chess piece. He wanted to play. Sort of.

"Come," Warner offered as if he were giving Sebastian a present. When Sebastian hesitated, Warner said, "Pisciculus knows he will lose so fast he will feel stupid and humiliated. That is why Pisciculus is afraid to play The Warner."

Warner often spoke of himself like he was talking about another person. And to show off that he was in the honors Latin class, he used Latin words a lot. Sebastian had to go online to find out that Warner had nicknamed him "little fish."

As Sebastian walked away, he heard Warner laugh sneeringly. Sebastian hadn't even played against Warner and he felt humiliated.

CHAPTER 4

After school the group of kids who sat with Lilly and Sebastian at lunch was going over to Josh's house to play a Wii game. They expected Lilly to join them, but she was going to tow her brother to the Chess and Checkers House for his lesson with Mr. Bernstein.

Sebastian protested that he was capable of getting there on his own. But Lilly knew her brother often took a wrong turn or was unaware of potential danger because he was lost in his daydreams. Those dreams were fun and magical and free from bad thoughts, except maybe about Warner.

Lilly saw a real world that besides sunshine and smiles had sharp edges and rainy days and disappointments and casually harmful stupidity. She wanted to protect the purity of her brother's innocence. At least as long as she could. So she would go with him.

Lilly knew her mom worried about her children being out and about in the city, although Jean thought that the neighborhood where they lived was no more dangerous than the suburbs or the country. There may be bad guys out there who could harm her children, but there were also policemen patrolling the sidewalks and streets. The parks were crowded with citizens whose presence and willingness to watch and call the police if necessary kept most of the criminals away.

It was in the dark and lonely streets where bad things could happen. That is where the rougher teenagers hung out and sometimes mugged the younger, weaker boys, taking their snack money or their phones or both. So Jean taught her children to avoid these areas.

Lilly and Sebastian always had cell phones to call for help if they needed it, and her thirteen-year-old daughter was wise beyond her age. Lilly had what Jean called "street smarts."

As Lilly towed Sebastian to his lesson, she knew from experience how to stay clear of the tough teenagers. She knew which sidewalks were free from the cracks that could launch Sebastian off his scooter or make her tumble off her skates.

She knew that what a person looked like and how they dressed could hide what they really were. She crossed the street to avoid a man in a downtown suit who talked to himself and angrily sawed the air with his arms. But she passed right by a homeless man dressed in ragged clothes pushing a shopping cart filled with cans and bottles. She had seen him around the neighborhood for years, picking through trash cans for the bottles he recycled at the food stores for five cents apiece. He was as gentle as a puppy.

Lilly and Sebastian climbed up the steps to the Chess and Checkers House, which was on a small hill. There were chess tables inside and many more arranged in a circle all the way around the building. Mr. Bernstein liked to play outside when it was sunny, and today the kids found Mr. B at his usual sunny-day place. Sebastian sat across the concrete chess table from him. Nearby, Lilly did her homework.

When Sebastian first took plates of food to Mr. Bernstein, he was a little afraid of the old man with the stooped shoulders and thin, white hair that was never combed. Old people could be really grumpy and sometimes they smelled funny. The old ladies with the bluish-white hair sometimes bumped into him with their carts in the supermarket and scolded him for being in their way, even if he had moved aside. Twice he and Lilly had stayed with their father's parents when Jean and their father had gone on vacation trips, and their grandfather was always criticizing Sebastian for not being neat enough or drinking his milk the wrong way.

Mr. B's eyes sparkled with curiosity. His voice was firm, with just a hint of an accent, like the European actors with good manners in the black-and-white films Sebastian's mother watched on the movie classics channel. He treated Sebastian more as a friend than some annoying kid who didn't know anything. Mr. B was Sebastian's favorite grownup.

Mr. B and Sebastian replayed a chess game between two Russian grand master champions, players so skilled that few others in the world could beat them. Mr. B took the part of one grand master and Sebastian the other. They followed each player's moves as recorded in the newspaper. "To be a champion chess player, you have to think and play like they do," Mr. B told his young student.

Mr. B asked Sebastian to explain why each player moved that specific chess piece to that specific square. Sebastian was not really paying attention. His thoughts were somewhere else.

Mr. B studied his student's face and realized he had seen this sadness before. "Did you play chess against Rude Boy?" That's what Mr. B called Warner.

"No," Sebastian answered.

"But you wanted to."

"I can't beat him, Mr. B."

"How do you know? You have only played against him once."

"He made me feel small and dumb. Smaller than I already am," Sebastian said. He didn't like being so short.

Mr. Bernstein closed his eyes and was quiet for a long time. Sebastian thought the old man might even have gone to sleep. Often when he brought Mr. B his dinner at night, he would find him napping in the big chair. Eventually, Mr. Bernstein opened his eyes and reached into the pocket of the brown suit jacket that he always wore. He pulled out a round object attached to a chain.

"Do you know what this is?" he asked.

Sebastian did not.

In his other suit pocket, Mr. Bernstein found his Metrocard. It was plastic, about the same size as a credit card. You had to use a Metrocard, which you bought from the station attendant or a vending machine, to get onto city buses or enter subway stations to ride the trains. "Before Metrocards we used these to pay for our rides. It's a subway token."

He handed it to Sebastian, who was still feeling sad and definitely not interested in old subway stuff.

"I've seen these, Mr. B. Mom took Lilly and me to the subway museum in Brooklyn. You used to put them in turnstiles to get into the stations."

He handed it back, but Mr. Bernstein didn't take it. "It's for you, Sebastian."

"Uh, thanks," Sebastian said without much enthusiasm. He liked it as much as he liked getting a pair of socks for his birthday.

"It's not just any subway token," Mr. Bernstein said.

From the tone of Mr. B's voice, Sebastian knew his chess teacher was about to say something important. He looked up at Mr. B's face.

"It can make you strong as you can be," Mr. B said, "but not stronger. And it can make you smart as you can be, but not smarter."

Sebastian inspected the token closely. It was round, about the same size as a nickel, and the color of dirty bronze. Its edges were smooth from years in subway riders' pants pockets and change purses and rattling into the subway turnstiles. In the middle there was a Y-shaped opening. Around that was written GOOD FOR ONE FARE. He turned the token over. On this side was printed NEW YORK CITY TRANSIT AUTHORITY. A chain connected to the edge of the token allowed you to wear it around your neck.

"It has magic powers, then?" Sebastian wondered.

"You already have the power. The token can help you learn how to use it."

"Thanks, Mr. B."

The old man smiled and said, "Goodspeed."

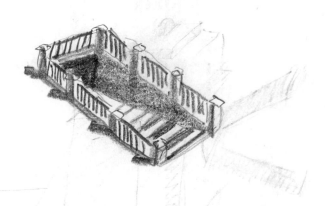

CHAPTER 5

"Goodspeed? What does that mean?" Lilly asked as she examined the token.

Lilly and Sebastian were setting the dining room table. Checkmate perched on Sebastian's shoulder. In the nearby kitchen, Jean cooked chicken cutlets and listened to her children.

"Mr. B says it is what adventurers wish for other adventurers when they start out on a journey. The wish is that the road ahead is not too rough, and if there is danger, that you will overcome it. Like if you were traveling on a sailing ship, the wish is that the wind would push you where you want to go and would not turn into gigantic storms to sink you."

29

"What's that got to do with a subway token?" she wanted to know.

"The person who discovered its power was an engineer on subways right here in New York. He drove the trains."

"Which subway?"

"The Number One. The A," he said, choosing two of the subway lines with stations in his neighborhood.

"You don't know, do you?"

"OK. He drove *a* train."

"Are you making this up, Seb?"

"Mr. B told me," Sebastian promised. "Mr. B doesn't know much about him, except that the engineer had a gold tooth right here." Sebastian pointed to one of his front eyeteeth. "He believed that everything we do is a journey or a trip. Going to the grocery store can be really boring, but if we keep our eyes and ears open to see and learn something new, then it's an adventure. Mr. B said if I was just a little bit daring, if I had a little bit of curiosity and nerve, my journey will take me to a new and exciting place where I can get stronger and smarter."

Lilly extended her arm, pointing the token at Sebastian. "If it has magic, then right now you would be a warty-covered toad."

"You tried to put a magic spell on me?"

"It's just a piece of metal. There is no magic in New York City."

Sebastian narrowed his eyes as he glared at his sister. He roughly grabbed the token back from her. "Mr. B wouldn't lie to me."

"OK, what powers do you now have you didn't have before Mr. B gave you that thing? Can you lift up the TV? Can you multiply three hundred eighty-four times six hundred ninety-two in your head?"

Sebastian knew he could not. He whispered something to Checkmate on his shoulder, then he looked at his sister and laughed.

"What's so funny?" she demanded.

"Checkmate says, 'Poppalooppa,'" Sebastian said. "Don't you want to know what that means?"

Lilly did not answer him. For someone who got very high grades at school, he could be so stupid sometimes.

"In squirrel talk it means my sister is a mean, ugly cow."

Lilly punched him hard on the arm, and he flinched.

"Enough, you two," Jean demanded as she brought out plates of food. "Can I see it, Seb?"

He handed the token to his mother.

"I used to have a whole change purse filled with these," she said.

"So there are more of them," Lilly said.

"There must be millions, maybe stored in a warehouse somewhere," Jean said. "Or there used to be. The city agency that runs the subways probably sold the tokens for scrap metal that could be made into something else."

Lilly shot a snide smile at her brother that said, "See."

Jean handed the token back to her son. "I don't know if this has magic or not. I'm a science teacher, so I believe in things I can see and touch and observe, like the laws of nature. But Sebastian, there are things called talismans. They are objects created by people who believe those objects have powers. If you believe — who knows?"

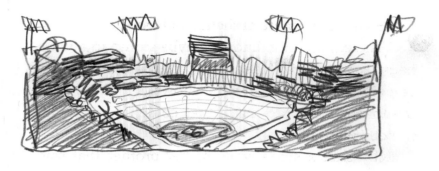

CHAPTER 6

"Sebastian," the voice called softly.

He woke up from a deep sleep.

"Hey, Sebastian!"

The voice came from outside. Sebastian climbed out of bed and went to the open window. He could hardly believe his eyes. Derek Jeter, the shortstop for the New York Yankees, sat in a bright red convertible parked right outside his building.

"Come on!" Derek called. "We have to go to the stadium."

"The stadium?"

"Yankee Stadium. Get some clothes on. We need you."

Sebastian stepped away from the window. His head spun. Was that really Derek Jeter? Did his favorite baseball player in the entire universe just ask him to come to Yankee Stadium?

Sebastian rubbed the token hanging around his neck between his thumb and his finger. Maybe. Maybe it had magic.

He looked out the window again. Derek beckoned him to the car.

Sometimes Sebastian was timid about going to new places or trying new things, but tonight he felt strong and safe. He was so excited that he got the buttons wrong on his shirt and had to undo them and then button them up again the right way.

Sebastian knew it was late at night, and he knew his mother would be very worried if she came into his room and found he wasn't in his bed. "Don't tell anyone, Checkmate," he whispered to his pet squirrel. As quietly as he could, Sebastian climbed out the window.

"You forgot your cleats!" Derek called out.

"I don't have cleats."

"Then get your sneakers."

Sebastian pulled himself back inside. His closet was such a mess he couldn't find his sneakers, so he grabbed his father's red ones he had saved from the trash. He slipped quietly out the window. Derek reached over to open the car door, and Sebastian hopped into the front passenger seat.

"How're you doing, Sebastian?" Derek asked in a friendly voice.

Very rarely did Sebastian have trouble finding words, but now that he was sitting right next to this great baseball player, his tongue was tied into a knot and he could not speak.

"Buckle up," the Yankee captain said.

Sebastian snapped on his seatbelt, and Derek roared down the street. Sebastian had never seen the city so quiet. He had been out late at night only a few times. Once when his parents were still married, they took him and Lilly to a late movie, and when they came out of the theater after midnight, the sidewalks were still filled with people and the roads were clogged with taxis and cars.

Tonight there were no people and no cars. Tonight the city belonged to Derek Jeter. And Sebastian Kemp.

Now he could answer. "Great! I'm doing great!"

Derek steered through a gate into a parking lot at Yankee Stadium, and they went in an unmarked door. Derek and Sebastian entered the Yankees' locker room, and Derek led him to a locker with Sebastian's name above it, right next to his own locker.

"Hurry. Put on your stuff," Derek said.

In Sebastian's locker was a New York Yankees uniform. This was all happening so fast, Sebastian did not have time to question why Derek Jeter would bring him to the stadium or what was going to happen next.

Sebastian put on the pinstriped jersey, which had the number 22 on the back, then pulled up the socks and the pants, which fit him perfectly. The red sneakers were way too big, but he laced them up very tightly so they would stay on his feet.

Derek handed him a bat and a helmet. They walked down a long tunnel to the dugout. Derek said, "You're up after me, kid."

"But I'm not very good," Sebastian said. "As a matter of fact, I stink. I'm always the last kid they choose for teams in phys ed class."

"You have to take a chance," Derek told him. "You can't get a hit unless you swing."

"But I might strike out."

"What's my batting average, Sebastian?" the future Hall of Fame player asked.

Sebastian knew many statistics about baseball and particularly about Derek Jeter. He knew Derek had a lifetime batting average of .314.

"You know what that means," Derek said. "For every hundred times I go to bat, I get only thirty hits.

The rest are pop-ups or ground-ball outs or strikeouts. You're the math whiz. How often do I fail?"

"Seventy percent," Sebastian said. Then he corrected himself as he did the math in his head. "Actually, sixty-eight point six percent."

"Anything that has real value or meaning is a challenge to reach, and you risk failing as much as sixty-eight point six times as you attempt to achieve it," Derek said with a smile.

Now he was serious. "So, if you don't even try, well, then you have already failed." He patted Sebastian on the back encouragingly and said, "Goodspeed."

Sebastian stared into Derek's face. If anyone had been on a journey where he'd discovered skills and inner strengths few people possess, it was the great Yankee shortstop. Had someone once given him the token?

Sebastian climbed the dugout steps and walked onto the field. He had been to several games with Lilly and their father, but he had never seen Yankee Stadium from the playing field. The stands were so high they seemed to reach up to meet the stars. He heard the buzz and hollering of the spectators. The grass was so green. The lights were so bright.

Sebastian practiced swinging a few times, then he took his batter's stance at home plate. He saw the pitcher throw the ball. He froze, unable to swing.

"Strike one!" the umpire yelled.

Sebastian had never seen a ball pitched so fast. He had no hope of getting a hit. Another pitch whizzed by him.

"Strike two!" rang in his ears.

Now Sebastian had only one more strike. If he swung and missed, he would be out. He would let the team down. He would disappoint his hero. He would fail.

Sebastian felt something warm on his chest. The token that hung around his neck seemed to be calling to him. He reached down and rubbed it between his thumb and fingers.

Then he gripped his bat tightly and swung as hard as he could at the next pitch. He smacked the ball. It soared into the outfield where no one could catch it. He ran to first base as fast as he could, and he ran and ran around the bases.

He never felt so free and joyful.

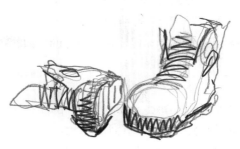

CHAPTER 7

S ebastian awoke in his bed and sat up immediately.
His head was filled with images of himself running around the bases at Yankee Stadium. He looked down and saw the red sneakers by the side of his bed.

"Yes," he said to himself and then called up to his sister in her bunk above him. "You awake?"

Lilly was almost always up before Sebastian, and, as usual, she was reading. He climbed up to her bunk and excitedly told her what had happened at Yankee Stadium. "It's all because of this," he said as he showed her the token on the chain around his neck.

"It sounds like a dream," Lilly said.

He knew she didn't believe him. "It wasn't a dream. Derek Jeter really did drive me to Yankee Stadium in a bright red car. The grass was so green. I clobbered a pitch a long way."

"You have wonderful, fantastic, colorful dreams, Seb. I wish I had dreams that real."

He pointed to his father's red sneakers. "Those were in the closet when I went to bed. How did they get there?"

"Maybe you moved them. You know you sometimes walk in your sleep," Lilly said.

Just a month ago, his mom found him wandering around the apartment in the middle of the night while he was sound asleep. She led him back to bed, and he never woke up until the morning. Later, she told him about finding him sleepwalking and that he had a flashlight in his hand. She guessed he was looking for something but he didn't remember sleepwalking or what he could have been trying to find.

Lilly's doubts did not shake Sebastian's belief that his baseball adventure was real. He felt strong and smart and ready for a challenge.

"Look out, Rude Boy. Here I come!"

CHAPTER 8

Sebastian studied the chessboard.

He had battled Warner for what seemed like hours, and it was still only lunch period. They had taken most of each other's castles, bishops, and pawns. The intensity of the players attracted some students and a few teachers who gathered around to watch. Sebastian had captured more of Rude Boy's pieces than he had lost. That he was actually going to win made his thoughts whirl.

Warner concentrated very hard. He wasn't his usual boastful self. He hadn't devoured any of his three cheeseburgers next to the chessboard. Sebastian moved his queen four squares. He was certain he set a trap for Warner that he couldn't get out of.

Warner leaned closer to the board, and after what seemed like half an hour but was only a few minutes, a cruel smile formed on his lips. He moved his knight and ripped the paper wrapping off a cold cheeseburger. He took a huge mouthful and spat out, "Checkmate!"

What? This was a move that Sebastian had not anticipated.

Warner took another huge bite. With his mouth full, the words came out as a mumble, but Sebastian clearly understood that he said, "The Warner is invincible!"

Up until this very last move, Sebastian was sure that today would be the famous day when he beat Rude Boy. He wanted to beat Warner as much as he wanted anything. Sebastian fought back tears. His eyes stayed dry but his stomach churned with anger and disappointment.

That night when he took Mr. Bernstein his dinner, Sebastian told him what happened. Mr. Bernstein didn't eat. He was more concerned about Sebastian's defeat than with feeding himself. He always had a chessboard nearby, and he asked Sebastian if he wanted to replay the game he lost to Warner to see if he could learn something.

Sebastian had a very good memory, and he recalled each and every move. Especially the one that beat him. He showed Mr. Bernstein how Warner placed his knight in a move Sebastian had not expected.

Mr. Bernstein stared at the chessboard and did not speak for a long time. He had a little smile on his face. Sebastian saw the smile, and it made him sad. Was Mr. B happy that he had lost?

But that was not why his teacher was smiling. "You don't like Warner, do you?" Mr. Bernstein asked.

Sebastian thought he might even hate Rude Boy. "No, I don't."

"And you were just about to beat him. You know that, don't you?"

"But I didn't."

It looked like Mr. Bernstein knew why.

"Maybe you were thinking how good you were going to feel when you checkmated him. You started celebrating your victory a little too soon, and you stopped concentrating on the game."

Mr. B was right, Sebastian knew. He'd been so eager to see the look of surprise and humiliation on Warner's face that he'd made a quick, stupid move.

"I can see from the way you played that you are no longer afraid of Rude Boy," Mr. Bernstein said. "That will make you smarter and stronger the next time you play him."

CHAPTER 9

The next day was Saturday, and a rematch would have to wait.

Sebastian used this time to sharpen his chess skills by studying more games by the Russian grand masters.

Lilly still wanted close-up photos that showed the snow leopard's fierce beauty, so she headed back to the zoo.

She had decals of white wings on her Rollerblades, and she loved to skate fast, even down the hills. Without towing Sebastian behind her, she sped along.

It was a glorious, warm spring day. Joggers of all ages, shapes, and sizes ran along the dirt track around the reservoir. Above them radiant white and pink petals blossomed on the trees. Lilly passed many other skaters, but the racers wearing tight, colorful racing suits zoomed by her. Some bicyclists seemed to fly along, while others panted up the hills, pedaling with all their energy. In the huge lawn called the Sheep Meadow, young men and women sunned themselves like they were at the beach.

One of the very few luxuries their mother bought for Lilly and Sebastian was membership at the Central Park Zoo. Lilly showed her membership card to the admissions guard and went right in.

The snow leopard was still nowhere to be seen, so Lilly sat down on the floor to wait with her camera ready. Next to her was a girl with unhealthy-looking pale skin drawing in a sketchbook. Lilly guessed she was probably a senior in high school or maybe in college. The girl wore a checked flannel shirt the same rust color as her hair. Her blue jeans had a hole at one knee. Her sneakers were old and scuffed.

At school Lilly couldn't dress like the rich kids with their expensive sneakers, Ugg boots, and trendy designer outfits they replaced with the latest styles every season. Some of the girls even wore silver or gold necklaces and bracelets from Tiffany on Fifth Avenue.

Lilly had her own look, made up of high-quality shirts and pants bought by Jean mostly at resale shops. Her mother described Lilly's style as "classic." The less kind girls in her class called it "on-sale" or "thrift-store" chic.

If anything, this artist's outfit came from the thrift-store reject bin. But there was one thing about her that was beautiful. Her drawing of the leopard's head. Lilly thought the big cat looked so sad that it was about to shed tears. Sad but glorious.

"That's..." Lilly was momentarily at a loss for the right word. "Beautiful," she said, pointing to the drawing.

The girl just shrugged.

"The leopard must have come out of hiding for you," Lilly continued.

"Not today," the girl mumbled.

Lilly was impressed. "You're drawing that from memory?"

The girl nodded.

"For a school project?" Lilly asked.

The girl laughed as though Lilly were really dumb. "I'll bet at the school you go to, you have lots of 'projects,'" the girl said.

Lilly was not sure if the girl was angry or just jealous. Lilly knew that going to private school was a privilege that few students in New York City could take advantage of. There were lousy high schools where teachers never required the students to do projects. Maybe the girl went to one of those.

Lilly didn't want to make the girl feel bad, so she simply said yes.

"That's what the camera is for, isn't it?" the girl said.

Lilly didn't know why, but she got the feeling that the girl was very smart. "I'm doing a science fair project on snow leopards, and I wish this one liked to have his picture taken."

"You going to be a scientist? Maybe a lawyer or a doctor?" the girl asked.

Lilly heard anger in her voice.

"I'd like to be a doctor," Lilly said. "How about you?"

"Where I come from, the kids grow up to be patients of doctors or gangsters defended by lawyers."

Lilly realized the girl most likely lived in a poor neighborhood in New York City where not many of the kids graduated from high school and fewer went to college and fewer still became doctors or lawyers.

Lilly pointed to the drawing of the snow leopard. "He looks so sad."

The girl turned toward Lilly. Her eyes widened with intensity, and there was fierceness in her voice. "It ain't free. It's locked up." She shook her head. "Girl like you skating around the city free as a bird soaring up in the sky, you don't know nothing."

The girl stopped drawing to watch a female zoo employee finish sweeping the exhibit floor. When the employee left, the girl jumped up, walked out of the exhibit, and vaulted over a little fence with a sign that read DO NOT ENTER. ZOO EMPLOYEES ONLY.

A few seconds later, the girl ran back. When she leaped over the fence, she dropped her sketchbook. A zoo employee was chasing her so she didn't stop to pick it up.

"She tried to let the leopard out of its cage!" the zoo employee yelled. "Stop her!"

The girl sprinted toward the exit. She was much faster than the guards. Lilly picked up the sketchbook but didn't have time to look inside. The snow leopard came out of hiding and appeared to stare right at her, almost as if it were posing. Lilly glided on her Rollerblades as close as she could get to the magnificent cat and took many pictures.

CHAPTER 10

Sitting at the dining room table, Lilly's mom admired the photographs of the leopard Lilly just got back from the processing lab.

Beside her, Lilly paged slowly through the sketch-book the girl with the rust-colored hair dropped at the zoo. The pictures on the left pages looked like an angry, brilliant child made them.

Most were done with brightly colored crayons. Some of these pictures portrayed a man and a woman, both about her parents' age, in horrible pain as a sea of flame burned them. A redheaded child floated above them with a curious smile. Lilly's parents were not religious, but she learned about heaven and hell from her grandmother, and this looked like the hell she described.

Other pictures showed the man and woman buried under piles of stuff that had wiggly lines coming off it to show how foul it smelled. Some drawings showed the child handcuffed to a pipe, frightened animal eyes in a half-seen face staring out of a darkened closet. No matter how crude the drawings were, Lilly felt the rage and fear that the artist portrayed.

Lilly thought a different person must have done the pictures on the right-hand pages. Drawn with an ink pen, they were so realistic that sometimes she felt she was looking at photographs. Every detail was perfect, and there were no cross-outs or do-overs. The artist had drawn them perfectly the first time. Here birds soared in cloudless skies. A child jumped happily on a bed. A young girl in a summer dress danced on a hilltop, her eyes bright with energy.

Further on in the book, Lilly found several drawings of a park with a tall monument that she did not recognize.

Only one picture covered both left and right pages of the notebook. In the realistic style, the girl had drawn the inside of what must have been a museum. On an exhibit wall were three pictures, and a young girl stood proudly off to one side. The middle picture on the wall was a much smaller version of the drawing of the dancing girl in the summer dress.

This image did not stir up the emotional reaction the other pictured roused in Lilly. But it did make her think. What was the girl's drawing doing in a museum? Was that her in the drawing, proudly viewing her work? Lilly thought that the girl artist maybe did have a dream. She didn't want to become a patient or a gangster like she predicted for many of the other kids in the neighborhood where she lived. She wanted her work to be good enough and famous enough to be in a museum.

"How can I take it back to her, Mom?" Lilly asked. "There's no name. No address. No phone number."

"Can I see?" her mother asked.

Jean studied the pictures, and her face hardened into anger. Lilly heard her mother curse under her breath, something Jean did very rarely. And her eyes were moist with tears. That made Lilly think her mother thought the frightening pictures on the left pages were, sadly, from the girl's actual experiences, not just from some dark imagination.

Lilly's mom recognized the tower. It was a monument to American soldiers and sailors killed fighting the British during the Revolutionary War in 1776. It was on the top of a hill in Fort Greene Park in Brooklyn.

"OK," Lilly said. "I'll take it to her there."

"No one lives in the park, Lilly. And anyway, you know Brooklyn is out of bounds."

"Will you go with me?"

"We don't know if she lives near the park. She could live anywhere and have just visited for a day or an hour. It would be a fool's errand."

Lilly was disappointed, but she knew her mother was very busy with her teaching job and taking care of her family. Trips, even adventures, that she judged would waste her precious time were fools' errands. The worst.

Lilly packed up her photos as Sebastian came into the room holding his squirrel.

"Checkmate is sure I'm ready to defeat The Warner!" he announced. He didn't get a response.

Sebastian looked back and forth from his sister to his mother. "Why are you crying?" he asked Jean. "What did Lilly do now?"

"Nothing." Jean forced a smile. "Nothing's wrong."

She reached out and put her arm around her son. "If Checkmate knows you're ready, then Warner beware."

CHAPTER 11

Classes were finished for the day, and most students were at various activities like band or the theater club or they were outside playing organized sports.

Warner was in the cafeteria playing against Mr. Kaveke, who taught physics in the high school.

Sebastian watched from the doorway. He smuggled Checkmate into school, and the squirrel now sat on his shoulder. Warner defeated Mr. Kaveke, and the teacher left the cafeteria by another door.

Sebastian was scared, and part of him screamed to just turn around and forget playing Warner. He rubbed the token between his thumb and forefinger. In his head he heard "You can't get a hit unless you swing." He marched over to challenge Rude Boy to a game of chess.

The match went longer than the one before. It took all of Sebastian's concentration, and in the end, he was the one who moved his queen to take Warner's king and win the match.

Warner was stunned. He had never lost to any student at Amsterdam Prep, and for once in his life, his appetite deserted him. He did not touch either of his two cheeseburgers next to the chessboard.

Sebastian grinned slyly at his opponent. "Little Fish says, 'Veni. Vidi. Vici.'"

Sebastian's father loved to study history, and Sebastian often watched the History Channel on TV with him. They saw a program about a general in the Roman Empire who, more than two thousand years ago, led his army into another country and conquered it. When he defeated the opposing army, he announced, "Veni. Vidi. Vici." Honors Latin student Warner would have no trouble translating what Sebastian told him: "I came. I saw. I conquered."

Sebastian rushed to the classroom where his mother taught science. At her desk Jean prepared the next day's lesson plan. Lilly was there looking at some caterpillars in glass jars her mother had collected to show her biology students.

Sebastian excitedly told them about his victory. "The entire chess club and Mr. Kaveke were watching, and when I checkmated Warner, they clapped and yelled my name and lifted me up on their shoulders and paraded me around the cafeteria and shouted, 'You are the champion!'"

Lilly and Jean gave each other a look. They both knew that Sebastian often fabricated his own reality.

"So you did beat Warner," Lilly said.

Sebastian hung his head like he had been defeated. "No."

No? Lilly was confused. She believed the part where he did play a chess match against Warner. She guessed that the part about the students parading him around on their shoulders didn't really occur. It was what he wished happened.

"Did you beat him or not?" Lilly asked.

"I didn't beat him," Sebastian laughed. "I crushed him. I humiliated him."

Jean swept her son into her arms and gave him a long hug. "Excellent," she said and kissed him on the cheek.

Lilly and her mother lifted Sebastian and his pet squirrel up to their shoulders. They marched out of the biology classroom into the hallway that during the school day was crowded. Now, after classes ended, only a few students and teachers were there to witness a beaming Sebastian and to hear Lilly chant "Here comes The Sebastian! Here comes the champion!"

CHAPTER 12

As soon as Jean and Lilly put him down, Sebastian raced out of the school building and scootered over to the Chess and Checkers House.

He was so eager to tell Mr. B that he didn't wait for Lilly to put on her Rollerblades and tow him. He only got lost once, and he scootered so hard he was out of breath by the time he got there. He found Mr. Bernstein at his regular outdoor chess table and panted out that he had beaten Rude Boy.

"Were you scared you would lose?" Mr. Bernstein asked.

"Yes."

"But you risked challenging him again. That's good."

Sebastian pulled the subway token out from underneath his shirt where he wore it around his neck. "Because you gave me this, Mr. B. It really works."

"It helped. But you were ready for an adventure."

Sebastian held up the token. "Did this make you a smarter chess player?" Sebastian asked.

"I needed something else."

"What was that?" Mr. B encouraged Sebastian to ask questions, even personal ones. He had once told him that caring for others, what he called empathy, and curiosity were the most important qualities a person could have.

"To discover how not to be lonely," Mr. B said.

After his wife died, Mr. B stayed in his apartment with the shades pulled down. He didn't read three newspapers every day. He rarely ate. He could hardly move from his big old chair, he missed her so much.

Sebastian missed Mrs. B too. He had really liked her. She was short like him, and she was always busy with some project. At Halloween she made bright green and red and yellow lollipops in the shape of knights in armor on rearing horses.

One year he had helped her melt the sugar and syrup and mixed in food coloring. Then they poured the liquid into metal molds the shape of the knights and put in sticks for handles. When the liquid cooled and hardened, they took off the molds, leaving the most wonderful lollipops.

Sebastian missed his father since he went to California, but he had Lilly and his mother and Checkmate around him, so he was not lonely. Mr. B was. Sebastian knew that his mother had been very concerned about him. She was not the only one.

"I was sitting in my chair with no lights on when the doorbell rang," Mr. B said. "It was Abdul. From the newsstand on the corner."

The newsstand was a little building on the sidewalk, although it was more like a shed than a building, where Abdul sold newspapers, magazines, candy, sodas, and cigarettes. Walking to school, Sebastian passed by Abdul almost every day. Abdul would wave and call out, "Assalamu-Alaikum."

Once, when Sebastian lost his apartment keys, Abdul invited him inside the newsstand to stay out of the rain. While he waited for Lilly or his mother to come by with their keys, Sebastian asked Abdul how to say hello where he came from in Pakistan. "In my language," Abdul had said, "you greet a friend with 'Assalamu-Alaikum.'"

Abdul was aware that Mrs. Bernstein had died. When Mr. B did not come to the newsstand for a month afterward, Abdul took Mr. B's favorite newspapers to him.

"Abdul saw that I had not changed out of my pajamas and was sitting in my chair with the shades pulled down. He saw uneaten food on the tray you must have brought the previous day. Abdul told me, 'Mrs. B has gone on her journey, and it is time for you to go on yours.' The next day he brought me newspapers.

"And the token. That is when I started on a new journey."

"You didn't go anywhere, Mr. B," Sebastian said. "You stayed right here in New York."

"The destination doesn't have to be Disney World or the beach." He touched his chest. "It can be searching inside for more strength or a new idea. Or it can be right next door." He smiled at Sebastian. "I found Lilly and your mom to cheer me up and to feed me. And you to play chess with."

So the token was not just Mr. B's. It had belonged to Abdul, who was from another part of the world where there might be real magic. On TV Sebastian had seen men who looked like Abdul walking barefoot over red-hot coals and making deadly cobra snakes sway calmly to music.

"Did Abdul bring it to America from Pakistan?" Sebastian asked.

"No. He was vague about who gave it to him or why, but he knew its history. The first person to get it was a boy just about your age who lived in Poland in Eastern Europe when a terrible war was going on. The boy and his parents were sent to a prison called a concentration camp where they were separated, and the boy's parents died there. American soldiers defeated the camp guards and freed the boy and the other prisoners.

"One of the soldiers gave him food and chocolate — what a treat that must have been for the boy who had been fed so little food his ribs showed through his skin. The soldier took him to an American base for homeless adults and orphaned children. Before he went back to fight in battle, he gave the boy his lucky charm, a subway token — the token you hold in your hand."

"Was that soldier the man who used to drive the subways in New York?" Sebastian asked. "The one with the gold tooth?"

"The same."

"What happened to him?"

"Nobody knows. He would be very old by now, older than me. He could have come back to New York City after the war to drive subway trains again. But I think he would have done something else, something where he helped other people more than just deliver them to work or bring them home on the train."

What Mr. Bernstein didn't say and sometimes feared was that the soldier had been killed in the war because he gave away his lucky token.

"So you started me on my journey," Sebastian said.

"And now it is time for you to find someone else who needs to be stronger and smarter. For the token to keep its value, you must pass it along."

"I can't do that," Sebastian protested. "How will I beat Warner again, Mr. B?"

Mr. Bernstein said, "You were always a better chess player than Rude Boy. You just didn't know it. You don't need the token any longer. You have its power now."

"I am pretty small, you know. I need it to get taller and stronger."

Mr. Bernstein shook his head.

Sebastian did not want to beg. He felt that if he did, Mr. Bernstein might think less of him, and Sebastian certainly did not want that.

"You have a very important job, Sebastian. First, of course, is that you want to be sure the person you give it to won't use the token to harm someone or something. There are many decent people who deserve help to become what they need to be or to overcome obstacles to accomplish their dream," Mr. Bernstein said. "Use your fine intelligence to find the right one.

"But also use your heart."

CHAPTER 13

S ebastian stood on the top of a large rock in Central Park and peered through the binoculars his mother used to study birds.

In the grass at the base of the rock, Checkmate sat on his hind legs. Earlier in the apartment, Lilly removed the bandage from his leg, and the wound appeared healed. She and Sebastian brought him to an open field near the boat pond to see if he could run. Checkmate was just sitting, so Sebastian scanned the park through the binoculars.

"What are you looking for?" Lilly asked.

"A person who needs the token," her brother said.

"Oh," she exhaled. *You have to learn that your made-up stories are not real*, Lilly thought. She did not say this out loud because she did not like to hurt her brother's feelings. Most of the time.

Sebastian spotted a young girl who was trying to ride a bike without training wheels but kept tipping over. Her father jogged alongside her to prevent her from falling onto the hard asphalt path. She got a little ahead of him, then tumbled to the pavement. She obviously needed the strength the token would give her. Before Sebastian could climb down from the rock to take it to her, though, she got up, wiped away her tears, and climbed back on her bike. This time she pedaled fast enough to stay upright, and she wobbled happily along the path.

Sebastian focused on a gray-haired lady sitting on a bench. She looked weak and tired, but she must have been just resting because she bounded up and jogged down the path.

On the Bow Bridge that gracefully arched across the boat pond, he saw a woman in a white wedding dress that glistened in the bright sun and a young man wearing a black suit. A photographer was trying to take their picture, but they were arguing. The man angrily turned his back to the woman, but seconds later he faced her and gently touched her cheek with his hand. She did the same, and they kissed for so long Sebastian thought they might not be able to breathe. They certainly didn't need any help.

Both Lilly and Sebastian heard a loud bark and saw a huge rottweiler straining against its leash. Its shaved-headed owner wore a shirt with no sleeves and had a thick muscular chest just like his dog. He didn't try very hard to keep the dog under control. It broke loose from his grip and raced toward Checkmate.

"Run, Checkmate!" Sebastian yelled with panic in his voice.

The squirrel ran, but because his leg was not 100 percent healed, he could not go fast enough to escape. The dog opened its jaws to crush Checkmate's spine, but in a flash a red squirrel ran between Sebastian's pet and the dog, distracting the rottweiler.

Now the dog chased the red squirrel. Sebastian couldn't be sure, but he thought the red was a female, and she was much too fast and quick for the dog. She zoomed this way and sprinted that way, then zipped up a tree.

Lilly scooped up Checkmate. "That red squirrel is fast."

Sebastian jumped down from the rock, and Lilly gave him the squirrel to hold.

The dog stood on its back legs with its front paws up against the tree, barking up at the red squirrel. The owner got hold of the leash and pulled the dog away.

Lilly walked directly up to the man with bulging muscles and shaved head. She was a hundred pounds lighter than him, and he could have bent her into the shape of a pretzel.

"You shouldn't have a dog if you aren't strong enough to control it," Lilly told him with no fear in her voice.

He scowled at her. "You shouldn't have a pet squirrel," he said. "It drives the dog crazy." He led the dog away.

The red squirrel came down from the tree and raced in circles around them several times.

"She's fast as lightning, Checkmate. She's Red Lightning," Sebastian said to his pet. "Go on. The red squirrel wants to play with you."

He put Checkmate down on the grass, and the squirrel ran cautiously toward Red Lightning. Even if his leg was totally healed, he would not be able to run as fast as the red squirrel. Soon he seemed to forget about his injury, and they played like puppies, tumbling over each other, running this way and that, and scampering up a tree to leap from one high branch to another.

Back at the apartment, Sebastian sat on the edge of the chair by the TV and stared at his mother through his binoculars.

At the dining room table, Jean edited a draft of a chapter she wrote for a biology textbook she and a science professor from Columbia University at 116th

Street and Broadway were going to publish. Sebastian said, "Mom."

She looked up to see him focusing the binoculars on her. "Is something wrong, Seb?"

"Nothing's wrong," he said.

He stared at her because he was considering whether she needed the token or not. She certainly didn't need to get stronger. The week before, she and Lilly had lifted a humungous air conditioner up from the basement storeroom. The machine was so huge that the building maintenance superintendent with the hairy hands wouldn't help them move it because he said it was too heavy. And his mother was smart enough that the university professor had invited her to coauthor the textbook. But maybe she wanted to be smarter.

Sebastian wondered aloud, "Mom, are you as smart as you can be?"

"I try very hard not to be dumb," she answered. "That's just as important as being smart."

"Can you multiply three hundred fifty-two times nine hundred thirty-three in your head?"

"Did you have another one of your fantastic dreams?" his mother asked. "Is that why you're asking me these questions?"

"I'm just thinking," he told her, and what he was thinking was that she probably didn't need the token.

In the bedroom Lilly glued her close-up photos of the leopard and pictures of the animal's jagged-peaked, mountainous habitat onto a poster board. At the center of the display was a map of central Asia, where the leopards lived.

Charts and pictures on a second poster told a disturbing story. Grinning native hunters crouched around leopards they had just killed. In his trophy room where he displayed the stuffed animals he had killed, an American hunter stood proudly next to a snow leopard with his cowboy boot on the animal's neck. Lilly had made a chart showing the population of the big cats one hundred years ago, then fifty, then twenty, then ten years ago. There were fewer and fewer leopards. Soon they could be extinct.

Along the edges of both boards, Lilly had taped carefully researched information about the scientific classification of the leopards (kingdom: Animalia; phylum: Chordata; class: Mammalia; order: Carnivora; family: Felidae; genus: *Uncia*; species: *Uncia uncia*), what they eat, how they live in such remote and barren environments, and how they raise their young.

In addition to the scientific information, she had a poem by English poet William Blake. It was about another large cat—a tiger, not a snow leopard—and to fully understand it, she had to look up some of the old-fashioned words, but it expressed the feeling of awe and power that the leopard inspired in her.

The Tiger

Tiger Tiger burning bright
In the forests of the night,
What immortal hand or eye
Could frame thy fearful symmetry?

In what distant deeps or skies
Burnt the fire of thine eyes?
On what wings dare he aspire?
What the hand dare seize the fire?

And what shoulder and what art
Could twist the sinews of thy heart?
And when thy heart began to beat,
What dread hand and what dread feet?

What the hammer? What the chain?
In what furnace was thy brain?
What the anvil? What dread grasp
Dare its deadly terrors clasp?

When the stars threw down their spears,
And water'd heaven with their tears,
Did He smile His work to see?
Did He who made the lamb make thee?

Tiger, tiger, burning bright
In the forests of the night,
What immortal hand or eye
Dare frame thy fearful symmetry?

Sebastian ambled in with the binoculars dangling on a strap around his neck. "First place, for sure," he said about her project.

"Hope so," she answered.

CHAPTER 14

S AVE THE SNOW LEOPARD the banner screamed in large red letters.

In the hallway near the main entrance to Amsterdam Prep, Monica Green had set up a display about snow leopards and how they were being hunted into extinction. It was almost exactly like Lilly's science fair project, only with much fancier and more expensive color posters and several computer displays with videos and web links to environmental groups trying to save the leopards.

Lilly came into school with her mother and Sebastian. The sight of the banner and display stunned her. She just stood there with mouth open.

Monica held out a coffee can into which students could donate money. "Do you want to contribute to my cause to save the snow leopards?" Monica asked Lilly. "Oh, that's right. You don't have any money." She smiled a viciously sweet smile.

Anger boiled up in Lilly so her eyes were burning fire like the tiger in the poem. Her body shook with rage. She tore down one poster and tried to yank the banner off the wall. A teacher pulled her away. "No Lilly!" the teacher warned.

Lilly ran out of the school. Jean and Sebastian chased her and called for her to come back, but Lilly kept running until she was out of sight.

Sebastian turned to his mother. "I think I know where she's going."

Lilly sat atop the rock she used to climb in Central Park when she was younger. She angrily wiped tears off her cheek. Lilly hated to cry and she hated Monica even more for making her cry.

Jean and Sebastian found her sitting there. The last time her mother saw Lilly cry was when Jean and Lilly's father separated and he left New York for California.

"Monica knew I was doing my science fair project on the leopards and how to save them, and she did that just to hurt me. The only way she has friends is to invite them to her gigantic townhouse or to pay for them to go with her to Broadway shows and expensive restaurants, and I'm the only girl in the class who is never invited," Lilly said angrily.

"If Monica did invite you, would you go?" Jean asked.

"Of course not," Lilly spat out. "She's a pig."

"Lilly," her mother scolded, "don't talk about people like that, even someone as cruel as Monica."

"Yeah, Lilly," her brother said, "don't call her a pig." Lilly glared at him. "Call her a fat, ugly, smelly, garbage-eating pig."

"Sebastian," Jean said firmly, but she couldn't hide a little smile. "Lilly, Monica is jealous of you. You both ran for class president, and Monica gave everyone in the class a present and you didn't, but you still won. You are good at soccer and great at your studies, and you make it look easy, even though I know you work really hard. Monica has to show you how hard she is trying in class or on the playing fields or at social events. The activity is always just about her. She is a self-centered, spoiled brat."

"That's all true, Mom, but now my project will look like I copied Monica, not the other way around. She is so mean."

Jean put her hand on her heart like it was aching. She knew that Lilly almost never whined or felt sorry for herself, but she knew that this disappointment and

75

the realization that some people were just plain cruel truly shook the way her daughter saw the world.

"The science fair is only a week away, and I don't have a project," Lilly said.

Sebastian took the token from his neck. He didn't need to look any further to find someone who needed and deserved it. He offered it to Lilly. "Here, you take this."

"I don't want that stupid thing," Lilly said.

"If you take it, I'll bet you'll think of a new project that will be better than Monica's," Sebastian said. "I beat Warner with it."

She grabbed the token from her brother and threw it into the tall grass.

Sebastian shot her an angry glare, but because she was so upset, he didn't say anything. He searched for the token in grass. And he searched, but he couldn't find it. Lilly came over to help. She saw tears streaming down Sebastian's cheeks.

"I'm sorry, Seb," she said.

"I can't lose it," he said. "I have to pass it on to someone who needs it. What will I tell Mr. B? He'll be so disappointed."

Lilly and Jean joined Sebastian on their knees, parting the long grass with their hands. Lilly cut her finger on a piece of broken bottle she did not see. It was not a bad cut, and she pushed the grass aside to find the glass to put it in the trash so no one else would cut himself or herself. And there it was. The token. She picked it up. A tiny centipede wriggled beneath it.

"I found it, Sebastian!" Lilly called out.

She held up the precious token for him to see. Sebastian was very relieved. She then bent down to pick up the tiny creature that was not more than half an inch long.

Jean knelt close to examine it. "I don't think I've ever seen a centipede this small," she said. "Isn't it amazing how a tiny creature like this could survive in the middle of New York City."

Lilly stared intently at the insect for a long moment then looked up at the tall skyscrapers that surrounded much of the park.

"Lilly, what are you thinking?" Jean asked.

This day, Lilly's plans and hopes for a great outcome in the science fair had been destroyed. She had been knocked down and she had a choice to stay down. Not every student entered a project in the science fair. There was no shame in just being a bystander.

But when she had been knocked down by a bigger player in a soccer game, her father, who was also the coach, urged her to get back up unless she was really hurt. Get right back up to prove to yourself you can

77

take adversity and to show the person who knocked you down that they can't keep you down.

"What are you thinking," Jean repeated, almost as if she were awakening her daughter from a daydream.

Lilly said, "I wonder how the little centipede got here?"

"An interesting scientific question that right now doesn't have an answer," her mother said in a tone that challenged her daughter.

"You have a new idea," Sebastian said. No more tears on his face now.

"Yes, and Monica won't be able to copy my new project," she said, but not with very much conviction.

"See what the token can do." Sebastian told his sister. He held it out for her take. She deserved it. "It will make you stronger."

Lilly put the token in the palm of her hand. It had almost no weight at all. Logically, it was just a round piece of metal. But her brother certainly believed that it gave him confidence and courage.

She nodded thanks to him and hung the token around her neck.

What Lilly discovered after many hours of research was that Central Park was a pretty nice place to hang out if you happened to be a centipede.

They like damp, dark places, like under fallen leaves or rocks, and there were plenty of both of those.

So a project about how a centipede lived there was nothing special.

But Lilly had not been able to find out was exactly what kind of centipede it was. She had read that there are over three thousand separate species around the world and she could not match hers to any others in the insect reference books she got from the New York City branch library on Amsterdam Avenue, near their building.

She decided to make her project about her search to identify the centipede and its origins. It wasn't a very exciting idea, but it was the best she had.

Using her mother's old laptop, Lilly searched Internet website databases of North American centipedes. She found no close matches to the bug she and Sebastian christened Ken, short for to*ken*.

While she hunted on the computer, Sebastian and Checkmate sat on his bed and he offered a Sebastian-ation explanation of the bug's origin.

In Central Park men with pushcarts sold soda, pretzels, and hot dogs. Some of the meat wound up in the trash cans or near them. There was a normal centipede that ate nothing but these hot dogs. He just loved hot dogs with or without mustard. Because of the chemicals and preservatives some hot dog makers put in their product, he mutated into a human-eating monster as big as the Empire State Building. Before he could eat all the people in the city, the air force dropped a huge bomb on him. The eight-hundred-foot-long centipede shattered into millions of tiny ones, like the little guy Lilly found.

Lilly had to laugh. Her brother might get a prize for creative writing, but not for science.

He fell asleep and she kept searching and searching. Her tired eyes ached and she was just about to give up and go to bed when she discovered a website about insects in Asia, or she thought that it was Asia. There was no writing in English, and the characters were like the ones she had seen on the menus from Chinese take-out restaurants. On this site she saw a picture of a centipede that was the closest to hers, tiny and pale yellow.

Jean came in dressed in her nightgown. "What are you doing up so late?"

"I'm trying to find out what this silly bug really is."

Jean looked at the screen. It went dark; she gently tapped it on the side and the image reappeared. "That looks similar to what you found," she said.

"But look at the writing. It's Chinese or Japanese, isn't it?"

"I'm not sure," Jean said. "So you think your centipede comes from Asia?"

"That's my hypothesis, my idea. But I don't know how to test whether I'm right or wrong."

Jean thought for a moment. "Remember Dr. Hoffman?" she asked. "We visited her laboratory in the research area of *our* museum. If anyone can identify what you found, she can."

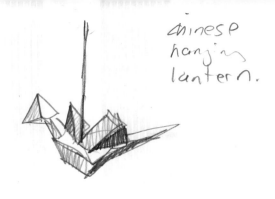

chinese hanging lantern.

CHAPTER 15

There were many great and famous museums in New York City, but the Kemps spent so many Saturdays exploring the exhibits at the American Museum of Natural History on 80th Street and Central Park West that they called it "our museum."

After school Lilly and Sebastian walked from Amsterdam Prep to the museum, climbed up the many front steps, and went into the huge Roosevelt Rotunda entrance. Lilly carried her prize in a glass jar with holes in the top for air.

Because they were on a scientific expedition, Dr. Hoffman had left them passes so they didn't have to pay the usual admission fee. They visited the museum so many times, they knew how to find Dr. Hoffman's laboratory without asking. They went through the North American mammals room to the elevators and took one to the fourth floor.

Dr. Ruth Hoffman met them at the door to her laboratory. The scientist was short with straight blond hair that she kept off her face with a clasp that was a copy of a big beetle. The round button on her white lab coat said DON'T BUG ME. Her eyes twinkled like she had just pulled a prank on someone, or was about to. When she gave both Lilly and Sebastian a welcoming hug, she smelled a little bit like chemicals.

At the corners of the museum, there were round turrets, and her laboratory was in one of them. Sunlight streamed in the large windows. A playful, brightly colored paper dragon lantern from lower Manhattan's Chinatown hung from the ceiling. Cabinets with pull-out drawers lined the walls. Jean had told her children that Dr. Hoffman had personally collected more than two thousand species of centipedes, one of the largest individual collections in the world.

"Want some chocolate?" Dr. Hoffman asked.

Lilly and Sebastian answered yes.

Dr. Hoffman offered them candy that looked like chocolate-covered raisins. Lilly and Sebastian each ate one. Something crunched when they bit down.

"What's inside?" Sebastian asked.

"Those are chocolate-covered ants," Dr. Hoffman said. "The ants are the healthiest part. Lots of protein."

Sebastian made a sour face, but Lilly just shrugged. The ant didn't taste bad at all.

"What have we got here?" Dr. Hoffman asked, peering at the centipede in the glass jar.

"We found this in Central Park," Lilly said.

Sebastian corrected his sister. "Lilly found it."

"It's a tiny little thing, isn't it?" Dr. Hoffman said. "Let's take a look under the magnifier."

She carefully took the insect out of the jar and placed it on a glass plate. She pulled over a large, square magnifying glass so they could see an enlarged image.

"How many legs does it have?" Dr. Hoffman asked.

Lilly had used her mother's magnifying glass to study the little creature and had counted the legs. "Eighty-two," she said.

Sebastian smiled. "One hundred sixty-four."

"Eighty-two pairs of legs," Dr. Hoffman said. "One hundred sixty-four legs. Hmmm," she thought aloud. "I don't know why they call these centipedes. How many legs does a centipede have?"

They both thought for a moment.

"One hundred," Lilly and Sebastian blurted out at the same time.

"That's right. *Centi* comes from the Latin language and means one hundred. This is an eighty-two-pede."

"I think it comes from China," Lilly said.

"That's your hypothesis?"

Lilly said it was.

"Let's see if you are correct."

Dr. Hoffman led them to a large cabinet and pulled out a drawer. In small, individual glass containers were hundreds of different centipedes. Dr. Hoffman selected a container and showed it to the kids. "I found this nannarrup in northern China ten years ago. It's very similar to Lilly's centipede."

"I saw one like that on an Internet website with Asian writing," Lilly said.

Dr. Hoffman put the Chinese centipede next to the Central Park one and studied them through the magnifying glass. They all agreed. They could see no difference between the two.

"So it's nan...?" Lilly wasn't sure of the name.

"Nannarrup."

"How did it get into Central Park?"

"Maybe at least one male and one female came in a shipping container from China that brought food for the animals in the zoo. Maybe someone bought a plant from China with the centipedes hiding in the potting soil and the plant was discarded in the park."

"It certainly looks identical. How can we prove it?" Lilly asked.

"Well, we can test DNA. That's the information in its genes, which are in the tiny cells in your body. The DNA determines who it is and how it grows and sometimes how it behaves."

Following Dr. Hoffman's instructions, Lilly helped take a tissue sample from Ken the Centipede to a laboratory in another part of the museum. In a large machine, a technician created a DNA identification that looked like the bar code on a quart of milk or peanut butter jar in the supermarket.

Then Lilly went back to Dr. Hoffman's lab, where special computer software compared Ken the Centipede's DNA against the DNA of the nannarrup from China, which was already stored on the computer. There were many similarities, but the centipedes were slightly different.

"What does that mean?" Lilly asked.

"They are cousins, not sisters or brothers," Dr. Hoffman said. "And that means, Ms. Lilly Kemp, that you have discovered the first new species of any animal in Central Park in over one hundred years."

"Look out, science fair," Sebastian almost shouted. "Here comes The Lilly."

The fair was only a few days away, and Sebastian helped his sister get ready.

He found a metal cookie tin and punched air holes in the side. He lined it with grass and leaves he gathered from the park and made a tiny tray for water. He used a rectangular magnifying glass he borrowed from Dr. Hoffman for the top. He and Lilly placed the tiny creature inside. Through the magnifying glass the half-inch-long centipede was an ugly critter with menacing claws for front legs.

"Nice," Lilly praised her brother. "Very nice."

She was not a hugging kind of sister, so she punched her brother affectionately on his shoulder. Sebastian was the hugging kind. He wrapped his arms around her and squeezed. Usually, she wiggled out of his grasp, but today she let him hug her until he wanted to let go.

While Sebastian and Checkmate slept on Sebastian's bed, Lilly made a slide show on her mother's laptop. It kept freezing; the picture program stopped working. Each time she had to turn the machine off and then restart it. It was past 1:00 a.m. by the time she finished her presentation.

Lilly climbed up to her bed. She was so excited about setting up her project the next day in the school gym, she thought she would be awake all night. She wanted to win first prize very much.

CHAPTER 16

A gleaming Apple iBook computer sat on a table next to a podium in the gym—first prize in the Amsterdam Prep Middle School science fair.

Lilly arrived carrying her display box, posters, and her mother's laptop computer. She wished she had that new one now. If her old piece of junk froze, she'd lose for sure.

She worked her way through the crush of students setting up their projects. The room was filled with parents and grandparents. Some of them hovered flinty-eyed near their children as if they were going to judge the judges who were judging their young stars.

Lilly was confident—until she saw Monica's project, a water-purification machine with a series of clear plastic tanks, hoses, pumps, and filters all connected in a big loop. Yucky-looking brown water started its journey through all this stuff and came out the other end crystal clear. Students and teachers gathered around to get a better look at how this marvelous contraption worked.

Lilly set up her display next to Josh Roberts, who had an exhibit on the physics of a baseball curve. He checked out her exhibit and wished her good luck. She wished him the same, although in her heart, she hoped he didn't have too much luck.

They both looked at Monica's water filter machine. "We don't stand a chance," Lilly said to him. "I'll bet her father made that for her."

Many parents of the seventh and eighth graders at Amsterdam Prep helped their children with their homework and science fair projects. Some helped a lot more than others.

Josh said, "Her father didn't build that thing."

"What do you mean? She never could make that herself. I'm in her chemistry class, and she is such a klutz she can hardly pour a liquid from one test tube to another."

"You know how Monica boasts about what an environmentalist her father is. He's building this huge skyscraper in midtown and it's supposed to be the most energy-efficient building in the city. They recycle water from the kitchens and bathroom sinks." He pointed at Monica's contraption. "With machines sort of like that, only a hundred times bigger."

Josh whispered into Lilly's ear, "The rumor is that her father paid mechanics from his skyscraper to make this machine. I saw Monica call someone on her cell phone to find out where the on-off switch was. She didn't even know how to turn it on."

Mr. Vanderhoff, a chemistry teacher from the middle school; Dr. Reed, a physics professor from Columbia University; and Mr. Frost, the president of a computer software company, were the judges. Lilly noticed that Mr. Frost looked like he was judging her mother rather than the exhibits.

Jean did not officially participate because she didn't want anyone to think Lilly had an unfair advantage with her mother as a judge, but she and her friend Dr. Hoffman were there to see all the exhibits and to root for Lilly. So was Sebastian.

Each exhibitor had five minutes to describe his or her project, and then the judges would ask probing questions.

Monica was ready. She wore a fancy dress, and she had her hair styled and blown dry—she looked like she was going to a prom, not a science fair. She answered the judges' questions with a wide smile. She posed just enough that Lilly could see Monica thought of herself as a star on a Broadway stage.

Lilly didn't like dresses, but no jeans today. She had on her best slacks and a blouse that actually matched. Neat, not fancy. As usual, she had her hair pulled back in a ponytail. Her only accessory was the token hanging around her neck.

When it was her turn to explain her project to the judges, she stammered nervously.

Standing close by, Sebastian motioned to her to rub the token with her thumb and finger. She made a face at him that said, "You have to be kidding!"

But she did it and took a deep breath to calm herself down. Now, she was able to look the judges directly in the eye and answer their questions in a steady, strong voice.

After evaluating each exhibit, the judges left the gym to choose who would win first, second, and third place. Jean, Dr. Hoffman, and Sebastian waited with Lilly, who thought it took the judges forever to decide.

Actually, they returned to the gym after only ten minutes. They gathered around a microphone.

Mr. Vanderhoff announced, "There are many excellent exhibits. Many more than we have awards for. Our decisions were not easy."

Lilly stood very still. "Please," she said to herself.

Sebastian saw the hope and anxiety radiating off his sister. She should be more confident now that she had the token and then he realized something terrible. He forgot to add the important inspiration "Goodspeed" when he gave it to his sister.

He felt like he was shrinking into a stupid creature the size of the tiny centipede, all intelligence and strength gone.

Mr. Vanderhoff continued, "The first prize for the annual Amsterdam Prep Science Fair goes to—"

He paused to build anticipation.

"Monica Green. Monica, come on up here."

Monica shouted a triumphant "Yes!" Her mother, father, and two sets of grandparents all gave her big hugs. Then she strutted up to the judges, who presented her with the Apple laptop computer. Lilly knew Monica already owned the newest, most expensive Apple laptop because she had lost two already this school year. Each time her parents bought her replacements.

Lilly was crushed. She wanted to win so badly. She had to force herself to smile when the judge announced that she won the second prize. Josh Roberts won third.

Lilly walked slowly to get her prize, which was definitely not a computer. It was a paper certificate. Mr. Vanderhoff told her that it was suitable for framing.

Her mother gave her a big hug. "I think yours was the best and most important project," she told her daughter.

"But you weren't the judge, were you, Mom," Lilly said angrily. But she realized it was not her mother's decision to award Monica first place. "I wish you were," she told her in a softer tone.

"I agree with your mother, Lilly," Dr. Hoffman said.

Sebastian knew what had happened. It was all his fault. He had messed up big time. No wonder Lilly didn't win. He hadn't done the transfer correctly. He muttered to himself, "I should have said it. I should have said it."

Then, without intending to speak out loud, he blurted, "I should have said goodspeed," with enough force that the people nearby heard and turned towards him. So did Lilly.

Voices buzzed with excitement as a television news cameraman and a female reporter entered the gym. The reporter asked Mr. Vanderhoff a question; the teacher pointed toward Monica and Lilly. Monica also saw the news crew, and she posed in front of her water-filter machine proudly displaying the laptop computer. She brushed her hair back and turned a little to her left. In pictures on her Facebook page and in school group photos, she always turned a little left because, as she informed everyone, her right profile was her best.

But the reporter marched right by Monica to Lilly and asked, "Are you the young scientist who found the bug that is the first new animal to be discovered in Central Park in over one hundred years?"

"Yes," Lilly answered.

"Do you usually cover middle school science fairs?" Jean asked the reporter.

"Never," she replied. "But when Dr. Hoffman called the station to lets us know about Lilly's discovery, the nanna-banana — "

"*Nannarrup hoffmani*," Lilly corrected. "Her scientist friends at the museum named it after Dr. Hoffman." She pointed to the scientist standing nearby.

"The *Nannarrup hoffmani*," the reporter repeated, "we knew this was an important story."

Jean whispered "Thank you," to her friend. Dr. Hoffman nodded with a smile.

Lilly could see Monica scowling right behind the cameraman. On the man's other side, Sebastian raised his fist in a victory salute. He was very happy for Lilly and very, very relieved he said goodspeed in time.

The reporter interviewed Lilly and then the expert, Dr. Hoffman, who wore a playful centipede brooch on her blouse. In the background Jean and Sebastian watched with delight and pride.

The story aired on the local news that night. One cable news network showed it to the entire country. So did an online news service.

The phone at the Kemps' apartment rang constantly for three days and nights as reporters called to do more news stories. A producer from *The Today Show* invited Lilly to be interviewed by Matt Lauer, but she would not go without her brother. The producer discouraged the idea until she found out that Sebastian had a pet squirrel that sat on his shoulder.

Jean came with them to the TV studio in Rockefeller Center. They brought Ken the Centipede in his tin box. Sebastian told Mr. Lauer that he and Lilly and Ken had been invited to go on *Sesame Street* but they didn't because birds like to eat centipedes and Ken was afraid of Big Bird.

Scientists from around the world called and mailed requests for Lilly to donate the little centipede to their universities or scientific institutes for further study. Some even offered to buy it. But she decided to give it to Dr. Hoffman at "her museum."

A week after the science fair and when the excitement with the newspapers and television reporters ended, the computer company president, Mr. Frost, called.

He explained to Jean that he was very impressed by Lilly's project. He wanted her to win, but he had been outvoted by the other judges. He believed there needed to be more women in the male-dominated world of science, and to encourage Lilly, he wanted to award her his personal prize.

Mr. Frost didn't get around the city in a car or a taxi or on the subway. He rode his sturdy old bike everywhere. He arrived at Lilly and Sebastian's building with a large box strapped to the back of it.

Jean invited him in, and he presented Lilly with a beautiful laptop computer. Lilly thanked him, then she and Sebastian explored the new laptop. Her computer-nut brother was impressed — it was loaded with cool, challenging math games.

Mr. Frost sat at the dining room table with Jean, drinking coffee she made for them. Lilly heard him tell her mother how he started a software business that was so successful that he had over one hundred employees working for him. To relax, he climbed really high mountains and explored jungles where no Americans had ever been.

Somehow he knew that Jean's husband was not living with her, and asked if she wanted to go out with him to a four-star restaurant Lilly once overheard Monica boast about going to.

Lilly was grateful he gave her the computer, but there was something about Mr. Frost that made her feel uncomfortable. Maybe because he only talked about himself and didn't ask Jean about what she was interested in or what music or books she liked. Lilly understood her mother's hesitation to go on a date with him.

Lilly wasn't sure if Sebastian whispered something in Checkmates ear or not, but she saw the squirrel jump up on Mr. Frost's lap. Checkmate never peed in the apartment, but he did today. Right on Mr. Frost's fancy blue jeans.

Lilly and Sebastian exchanged a look which said: I guess Checkmate was not charmed by Mr. Frost, just like their mom.

When he left the apartment, Mr. Frost glared at the beautiful laptop. Lilly was sure that he was angry he gave it to her and wanted to take it back.

CHAPTER 17

The next day Lilly woke up early, as usual. What was unusual was that Sebastian was not still asleep in his bed. He sat at the open window, looking out through the binoculars.

"Hey, Seb. I had a dream," Lilly said.

"Yeah," he replied uninterestedly. "The token has dreams in it."

Lilly had forgotten she had the token around her neck. She wondered—could this really make her dream?

Sebastian handed the binoculars to Lilly. "You need these now."

"For what?"

"To find someone to give the token to. Maybe you didn't win the science fair, but you did go on an adventure and discovered a new species. Now you have the token's power, and Mr. B says that you have to pass it on to someone who deserves it."

Lilly took the binoculars, but she wasn't about to go out on the street to find someone right now. She was too excited.

She found her mother curled up in one of the old chairs by the TV, reading the Sunday *New York Times*. "Mom, I had a dream last night!"

"What was it about?" Jean asked.

"I...I'm not sure. Some people were in a crowded room. I couldn't make out their faces so I don't know who they were, but they were dancing together or doing something fun. It's the first dream I've ever had!"

"We dream every night," Jean said. "Some people remember every single dream like it was a colorful movie. Your brother is the number one example."

"Dreaming. Very cool," Lilly said and made herself breakfast of cold cereal with cut-up banana on top.

Sebastian slumped in looking sad and worried. "Mom, have they caught the coyote in Central Park yet?" he asked.

"I don't think so." Jean closed the newspaper. "There was nothing in today's paper about it."

Sebastian hung his head. "Checkmate went out the window yesterday afternoon to play with Red Lightning and didn't come home. I think the coyote got him."

"Don't be silly, Sebastian. Checkmate is your pet, but he isn't like a dog or a cat. He's not domesticated like they are. Squirrels are wild animals. He's probably just out in the park somewhere gathering up acorns for winter or playing with his friend."

"Oh man, I think the coyote got him," Sebastian repeated in a sad voice. "I think Checkmate's gone forever."

"I saw on the TV news that some of the policemen who patrol Central Park think it could be a stray dog that looks like a coyote," Lilly said to ease her brother's concern.

"Now you're the one making stuff up," he said to her. "And anyway, dogs go after squirrels too."

"I know Checkmate is out there somewhere. We'll look in every tree and bush in Central Park until we find him," Lilly promised her brother.

Sebastian wasn't sure he believed her. And besides, it was pouring rain outside.

A little wet weather could not stop Lilly. Once she made up her mind, she was very determined.

Wearing long raincoats with hoods and big rubber boots, she and her brother went out into the rain. They started their search at the south end of Central Park near the Plaza Hotel on 59th Street. When they couldn't locate the squirrel there, they went north, heading past the Central Park Zoo to the boat pond. No one was out rowing the sturdy aluminum boats because of the bad weather. Lilly and Sebastian went over the graceful arch of the Bow Bridge into the hilly woodland area called the Ramble.

There were so many trees. So many bushes. Checkmate could be curled up in any one of them trying to stay dry. They called his name and heard no answer. No wet, scared squirrel scampered down a tall oak tree to them.

Sebastian was tired and hungry and wanted to go home. Lilly was not ready to give up. She carried him on her back for a long while.

Further north, close to the city parks department's Lasker swimming pool, they followed a dirt path into an area called the North Woods that looked like a wilderness forest hundreds of miles distant from the concrete sidewalks and huge buildings of New York City. Lilly and Sebastian trudged tiredly along, calling out for Checkmate.

Suddenly, an animal ran out of a dense thicket of bushes and stopped right in front of them, baring its teeth.

This was the wildest, dirtiest, smelliest, creature Lilly had ever seen. It was so skinny its ribs showed through its filthy, wet fur. Part of one of its large pointed ears was missing, like another wild beast had bitten it off in a fight. Yet, she was not afraid, and she did not know why.

"It's the coyote," Sebastian choked out. "He's going to attack us!"

"No," she said calmly.

Was this a wild coyote that had lost its way in the suburbs and undeveloped land surrounding New York and somehow wound up in Central Park? Or was it an abandoned dog? Lilly took a half step forward with the back of her hand outstretched to the animal.

"It's OK," she said.

She stepped closer so it could sniff her hand. Whatever it was, it stopped growling and showing its fangs. It whined a little.

"He's telling me that he's a stray dog," Lilly said, "and he's afraid that if the park police catch him, they won't put him in a zoo. They'll destroy him."

Sebastian was astonished. "He's talking to you?"

"Yes."

"You must be making it up."

The animal whimpered.

"See? He said he likes you," Lilly said.

"You sure you're not making it up?" Sebastian questioned.

"You can hear Checkmate when he talks to you. I can hear the dog."

Lilly stepped closer to the animal and petted it on the head.

Just then, two Central Park policemen in green raincoats came running along the trail. The man with gray hair was breathing hard from chasing the animal. The other one carried a big rifle and pointed it at the beast.

"Get away! The coyote could attack you and it could have rabies," huffed the older policeman.

Both Lilly and Sebastian knew that rabies was a disease that made animals crazy. If the beast had rabies and bit them, then they would become crazy too.

Lilly kept petting the beast's head. "This is my dog," she told the policemen.

"That's a coyote," the one with the rifle said.

"I know it looks like a coyote, but it's a mix-breed mutt. We got it at the animal shelter," Lilly said. She wasn't as good a fibber as her brother, but she had to save this animal.

"What's its name, then?" demanded the older park policeman.

"Lady," said Sebastian.

"Lucky," said Lilly at the same time.

"Lucky or Lady?" the policeman challenged them. "That's not your pet. You don't even know its name."

"It's Lady-Lucky, sir," Lilly said politely.

She could see that the policemen did not believe her. The one with the rifle still had it pointed at their "pet." Lilly had to do something bold.

She addressed the animal. "OK, Lucky, roll over." She quickly remembered its real fake name. "Roll over Lady-Lucky."

If this beast was a coyote, it wouldn't understand her. If it was a stray dog that had once been someone's pet, it may have learned this trick. But it just stared blankly at her. She repeated the command to the animal. It did not move.

"Get away," the policeman with the rifle commanded. "I'm going to shoot it."

Lilly looked the animal in the eye and, in desperation, rolled her hand in a circle to show it what she wanted it to do. She held her breath for a long, long moment.

The beast rolled over on its back. Lilly knelt beside it and rubbed its smelly, filthy stomach. This had to be a dog. It understood her command, and dogs love to have their bellies rubbed.

"Good dog," Lilly said.

The policeman lowered his rifle and said with disbelief, "Lady?"

"It's a male!" the other policeman declared.

With the animal lying on its back, everyone could see that it was definitely a male, not a female.

"We're just kids," Sebastian said with a straight face. "What do we know?"

"Your 'dog' doesn't have a collar or a New York City dog license," said the policeman. "I should give you a ticket."

"We're looking for his collar, sir. It's bright blue."

"With pictures of dog bones on it," Lilly added

"That's why we're in these woods. An animal bit is collar off," Sebastian said, pointing to where the fight supposedly took place. "I'll bet that was a coyote. It looked very much like our dog, only meaner. It had evil eyes and bloody fangs this long." He held his hands about a foot apart to show the policemen how huge the fangs were. "He was going to attack us, but our dog saved our lives. Lady-Lucky always protects us and...," Sebastian went on and on.

These policemen had heard many dumb excuses and fibs and made-up stories from New Yorkers and tourists who were caught doing things they shouldn't be doing in the park. Lilly could tell from the expressions on the policemen's faces that they knew what Sebastian was telling them was a big fib. She figured it wasn't a big enough fib for them to bother about. They shook their heads in disbelief as they walked away.

Lilly and Sebastian were soaking wet. They were exhausted from searching the park from bottom to top and did not have the energy to keep looking for Checkmate. They headed home. And the dog followed them.

"You can't come home with us," Lilly said to the animal.

Sebastian said, "He's so wet and looks so hungry, he needs a place to stay."

"When Keye died, Mom said no more dogs."

For years they had a dog they got at a shelter whose fur was all white except for a black circle around one eye. It looked like he had gotten a black eye in a punching fight, so their dad had named him Black-eye, or Keye for short.

The dog kept following them.

"Go on, now," Lilly told him without much conviction.

The dog hung its head. Its tail dropped down between its back legs. Their mutt Keye taught Lilly and Sebastian how to understand a dog's feelings or thoughts by interpreting its physical acts. They knew the miserable creature was as miserable as he looked.

"What if we bring him back to the apartment just until it stops raining?" Sebastian asked.

Lilly was thinking. Their mother often went to yoga class on Sunday afternoon. Maybe they could sneak the dog in and out before she returned.

"He looks like he's starving. You can see his ribs right through his fur. We need to feed him too," Sebastian said. He made two sounds just like a dog's whimper, and Lucky echoed the sounds back to him. "He says that he's dreaming of a nice, warm apartment so he doesn't have to scrounge for food in garbage cans and sleep out in the wet, cold park."

"He said this to you?" Lilly asked.

"Didn't you hear him?"

"Of course I did," Lilly said.

"He's like the Big City Coyote, only he's a nice dog."

"I'll bet Big City Coyote never smelled this bad," Lilly said. "He'll stink up the entire apartment."

"Then we'll have to give him a bath."

CHAPTER 18

The stray mutt sat perfectly still in the partially filled bathtub.

Sebastian had poured on so much shampoo that the dog looked like he was coated with a thick layer of whipped cream.

"No," Jean said firmly. She stood in the bathroom doorway, a scowl on her face, her arms folded across her chest.

"Mom, you know most dogs hate getting shampooed," Lilly said, "but he's sitting so calmly. It even looks like he's smiling."

"Dog's don't smile," their mother informed them.

"Why can't we keep him, Mom?" Sebastian asked.

"There is no room in this small apartment for such a big dog and we have no room in our budget to buy dog food."

"What if we pay for his food and collar and everything?" Lilly offered.

"You know," Jean explained, "owning a dog in the city is a lot of work. It isn't like having a pet in the suburbs or the country where you just open the back door and let the dog go into the yard. You have walk it in the morning and the evening even when it's raining or snowing or it's ten degrees below zero so the dog can pee and poop. And so people don't step in the poop you have to put it into plastic bags and then toss the bags in a trash can. The dog looks like he's less than two years old, and young dogs need exercise. You'd have to give it enough time in the park so he could run."

Almost as if they were singing a duet, they replied together, "We'll do everything."

"He seems sweet," Jean said. After a long, thoughtful pause, she said OK.

"Thanks, Mom," they both said.

"What's its name?" Jean asked.

"We decided on Lucky," Lilly said.

Jean smiled. "He is lucky you found him. I guess you two will find out if you still feel lucky you found him after taking care of him for a while."

CHAPTER 19

Lilly always walked Lucky before school and on weekend mornings.

This morning when she led her dog out the front door of her building, she conjugated irregular verbs in her head to prepare for a quiz in Spanish class instead of being aware of her environment like she usually was.

"You got it?" the voice demanded.

Startled, Lilly looked up. The sun was still low in the sky, and it shone right into her eyes. She couldn't see the face of the hulking figure in front of her.

"You got it?" the person repeated.

Lilly shaded her eyes and saw the girl with the rust-colored hair. "You're the girl from the zoo. You dropped your sketchbook."

"Yeah. The girl from the zoo. You got it?"

Street talk, Lilly thought. She had heard it before, not so much in her school, but on the sidewalks and in the playgrounds where the neighborhood kids played basketball. Don't show weakness. Be bold. Be in your face.

But Lilly was not threatened. Nor was Lucky, who bared his teeth and growled if anyone looked sideways at Lilly or Sebastian when they were out on the street or in the park. The girl's words were tough, but the way she said them was not.

"I have it," Lilly said. "I wanted to bring it back to you, but there was no name or address in it. I—"

"I'll take it," the girl said.

Lilly and Lucky went inside. Lilly returned a moment later and handed over the sketchbook.

The girl thumbed through it, as if she were making sure Lilly had not ripped out any of the pages. She sighed in relief. "Thanks," she mumbled.

"You make wonderful drawings," Lilly said.

The girl with the rust-colored hair didn't say anything, but she didn't leave either.

"How did you find me?" Lilly asked.

"You're famous. I saw you and your bug on the TV."

Now Lilly didn't have anything to say.

"When you're a rich and famous doctor living in a penthouse, you'll have to buy one of my drawings," the girl said.

"Who knows if I'll be famous or rich," Lilly said.

The girl pulled a piece of paper out of her jeans pocket. "I know."

She handed Lilly a new version of the drawing where the girl was looking at her own artwork in a museum, only this time the picture in the middle was not of a girl dancing but was an excellent portrait of Lilly looking a little older than thirteen and wearing a white lab or doctor's coat.

"Thank you," Lilly said. "I'm Lilly."

"I know who you are."

"What's your name?"

The girl's voice was almost a whisper. "Norma."

And then she walked away.

"Wait, Norma!" Lilly called. She wanted to invite Norma in the apartment to talk to her. Maybe they could become friends.

But Norma kept walking, not even looking back.

CHAPTER 20

Sebastian walked Lucky after school or in the early evening, and Lilly often went along.

They took their dog to a field not far from the 77th Street park entrance where many owners who lived on the West Side brought their pets. The grownups socialized or drank coffee or looked at their phones or did all three while their dogs of all shapes and sizes played. Lucky liked to chase a young golden retriever around the edge of the field.

Lilly brought the binoculars to search for someone who needed the token. But before she could focus in on any one dog owner or jogger or the moms pushing complicated baby strollers, she saw something red flash high up in a tree. She looked up and discovered

Red Lightning perched on a branch next to a gray squirrel that she guessed was Checkmate.

She shouted to her brother, who came running over, delighted to see the squirrel alive and well. He called to it, but it would not budge. Lilly knew why. It was because of Lucky. Dogs love to chase squirrels, and bad things happen if they get caught.

Lilly snapped the leash to Lucky's collar. "If you can get Checkmate to come down, then we can introduce him to Lucky," she suggested to Sebastian.

At the base of the tree, Sebastian pulled a plastic bag of dried cranberries out of his pants pocket and put some in his hand. Checkmate scooted down, snatched a treat, and quickly retreated, but not all the way to the top. Sebastian talked to him in a gentle voice, and eventually Checkmate allowed Sebastian to hold him.

Lilly bent down on one knee so her face was close to Lucky's. "See, Lucky, Checkmate is one of us. He belongs to our family, our pack." She knew dogs are very loyal to their pack. He appeared to nod his head in agreement. She smiled and called over to her brother, "Lucky says he will not hurt Checkmate."

"I didn't hear him," Sebastian said.

"Trust me. Trust Lucky."

Lilly walked Lucky toward her brother, who held his pet. The dog did not strain against the leash like he wanted to attack the little animal. His tail wagged.

But as soon as Lucky got close, Checkmate jumped out of Sebastian's arms and zipped up the tree.

"Checkmate didn't believe Lucky wouldn't hurt him," Sebastian said.

Lilly didn't want to be mean, so she said this as kindly as she could. "It was you who didn't believe. Checkmate knows what you feel."

On the way back to their apartment, Sebastian held Lucky's leash. They passed a squirrel near the asphalt path and Lucky jumped at it, almost pulling Sebastian over. The little animal escaped up a tree.

"See?" Sebastian said. "Lucky *hates* squirrels."

"That one was not a member of our pack so he had to go after it."

Sebastian thought his older sister might be right about their dog, but he was not about to admit that she was right and he was wrong.

That night he put a handful of dried cranberries on the window ledge, hoping that the squirrel's craving for the treat might lure him back to the apartment.

Lilly woke up early and climbed down from her top bunk.

The cranberries on the windowsill were gone. Sebastian sat cross-legged on his bed petting Lucky, who was curled up beside him, his eyes open and his tail wagging in a slow friendly beat. Right in front of his snout, Checkmate sat up on his hind legs eating the last dried cranberry. He had come in the open window during the night. When Lucky didn't growl or chase him, the squirrel must have realized that the dog recognized that he was one of the pack.

"See?" Sebastian said with a grin. "Lucky *loves* squirrels."

Checkmate was just a little squirrel, so he didn't eat very much. But Lucky did. Maybe because when he lived in back alleys and the park, he never got enough food. Now, he ate whatever they put into his bowl and asked for more.

And he ate one of their father's red running shoes he pulled out of Sebastian's closet. He didn't eat it, really. He mostly chewed on it. Lilly and Sebastian thought their mother would be angry, but Jean was not annoyed, just puzzled.

"I thought I threw his dumb sneakers out a while ago." A sly smile came to her face. "It's a good use for them."

Lilly and Sebastian earned a small amount of money doing chores around the apartment: washing the dishes, taking out the garbage and the recycling, making their own beds, helping with the cleaning and food shopping.

That was not enough to pay for all Lucky devoured. They both had saved part of the money they received on their birthdays from their grandparents, but that was soon gone. They had to go to work.

Sebastian made posters advertising his skills as a computer expert and taped them to streetlight poles and bulletin boards in the neighborhood. He got calls from several older people, one of whom he was able to help. The woman thought her computer was broken, but it just needed to be plugged in. So he earned one fee. With the two other appointments, he never made it past their entry doors. When the potential customers saw that the "expert" was a short, eleven-year-old boy with a squirrel perched on his shoulder accompanied by a large animal that looked suspiciously like a wolf or a coyote, they would not let him in.

Lilly told families with young children in her building and in other apartment buildings on her street that she was available for babysitting. The couple who'd moved into the apartment on the sixth floor where she and her family used to live had a four-year-old boy named Randolph, and they hired Lilly to "interact" with him while they were out shopping for a larger apartment.

To his adoring parents, Randolph was the perfect child. To Lilly he was a perfect brat. He threw screaming tantrums when he didn't get what he wanted immediately—and what he wanted was ice cream, soda, and candy. He actually kicked her when she was slow in scooping out half a carton of double-fudge cookie-dough vanilla ripple into a bowl bigger than Lucky's food dish. After that one very long afternoon interacting with the brat, Lilly told the parents that she was no longer available. No one else called.

Lilly and Sebastian were worried. They had no idea how they were going to earn the money they needed to buy dog food. Returning with Lucky after walking him in the park one afternoon, they met Miss Flannigan as she left the building. She dyed her hair a different color almost every week. Today it was fire-engine red.

"That dog," Miss Flannigan said. Sebastian thought she sounded like the witches on the TV cartoons. She pointed her cane like a weapon at Lucky. "He barks and growls when anyone comes near your door," the old lady said.

"I'm sorry if he makes too much noise, Miss Flannigan," Lilly said sweetly.

"Sorry? I'm the one who is sorry. I wish I had a dog. He would scare the robbers away when they came to steal what they didn't steal before."

And that is when Sebastian came up with an idea. Miss Flannigan's doorbell had not worked for many years. The building's superintendent with the hairy hands who was responsible for keeping the building in working order never got around to repairing it.

Sebastian asked Miss Flannigan if she would like it if he repaired her doorbell. She agreed and said she would give him "a little something" for mending it.

Sebastian disappeared into his bedroom with Lucky and Checkmate and closed the door. He had a natural talent for fixing and making mechanical and electrical things, and he spent hours and hours at his desk putting parts together. He and Lucky went to the local RadioShack electrical supply store where he used his last $11 to buy more parts. Then he went back to his cluttered desk.

From behind the closed door, Lilly and Jean heard Lucky barking the meanest bark they had ever heard their sweet dog bark. They questioned Sebastian about what he was creating. He smiled and would not tell.

After a few days, Sebastian emerged with his doorbell and asked Lilly to help him install it at Miss Flannigan's. That meant they had to go into her apartment.

She unlocked all four locks to let them in. Today she had dyed her hair bright orange, so when the light hit it, it almost looked as if her head were on fire. Inside, all the windows were shut tight and protected by metal security grates. The air smelled old and stale. Everything in the apartment was old: the chairs, the sofa, and the TV in a wood cabinet the size of a compact car.

The existing bell was above the apartment entry door. To reach it, Sebastian had to stand on four telephone books stacked on a chair. Lilly supported him so he wouldn't fall while he unscrewed the old, dead doorbell and replaced it.

"Would you like to try it, Miss Flannigan?" Sebastian asked.

"Certainly," she replied.

She was surprisingly quick and zipped over to her front door. She did not need her cane to walk. She carried it as a weapon to defend herself in case the robbers broke in again. She pressed the doorbell. There was no sweet chime. There was no irritating buzz. What she heard was a dog barking fiercely, then growling, then snarling even more ferociously. She stopped pressing and then pressed again to make sure the barking came from the doorbell.

Miss Flannigan laughed. It was not a witch's cackle. It was a joyous, wonderful laugh.

"You are a genius, young man." She never remembered Sebastian and Lilly's names. "That barking would scare the devil himself. Would you two like a soda pop?"

They both said yes. Their mother did not allow colas or sugary drinks in their apartment, but still, they both liked them every once in a while.

"Look in the icebox in the kitchen." Even the words Miss Flannigan used were old.

Lilly and Sebastian went into the kitchen. "What's an icebox?" Sebastian asked in a quiet voice.

Lilly pointed to the refrigerator and her brother nodded. Inside, the shelves were filled with cans of black cherry cola. The only food was several containers of cottage cheese with pineapple.

When they came back from the kitchen, Miss Flannigan was holding a heavy velvet bag tightly in her fist. She opened it on a table, and silver coins spilled out.

"I hid these so well the robbers didn't find them," she said. She picked one up and held it to the light so it glistened. "John F. Kennedy silver half dollars minted in 1964. He was a great president of the United States when I was a young woman. Tragically, he was assassinated."

She gave Sebastian and Lilly five shiny half-dollar pieces each. "You made me laugh today. That hasn't happened in a long, long time."

Sebastian hid his disappointment. Her idea of "a little something" was pretty little. Ten half dollars was only five dollars total. He had spent more than that on the doorbell parts.

"Thanks," they both said with as much fake gratitude as they could, which was not much.

"In a perfect and just society, there would be no reason for citizens to be fearful," Miss Flannigan said. "But we do not live in such a world. Many of my friends are old and scared, and they would feel more secure if they had a wonderful barking buzzer, so, I'll become your representative. I'll sell your wonderful device to them, and I'll make sure the old skinflints pay you full price."

"That's great, Miss Flannigan," Sebastian said.

Lilly spoke up for her brother. "What do you think the skinflints will pay, Miss Flannigan? Sebastian spent eleven dollars of his own money to buy parts for the doorbell."

Miss Flannigan understood Lilly's intention. "Some things in this world have more value than what you see on the surface. The United States Treasury will never make more Kennedy halves, and because there are more coin collectors and dealers who want to own the coins than there are coins available, their value has increased. Mr. Gold knows just how much more. He owns the Coin and Stamp Collectors Shop on 78th Street, down the stairs in the basement, and he will buy them. Tell him to be fair or he will have to answer to Red Mary."

They guessed that is what the store owner called Miss Flannigan because of her hair color, although today she would be Orange Mary.

Sebastian thought it was funny that the owner of the Coin and Stamp Collectors Shop who would buy the silver coins was named Mr. Gold, not Mr. Silver.

He offered them $16 for each of their ten half dollars. The kids were surprised and elated. $160!

With that money and profits from the barking-dog doorbells they sold and installed for Miss Flannigan's skinflint friends, Lilly and Sebastian had more than enough money to feed their dog and even to buy him some special treats.

CHAPTER 21

"Use the token," Sebastian joked as he and Lilly climbed onto the Number 5 bus on Broadway.

They were on their way to their dentist's office on Fifth Avenue near 46th Street. Of course Lilly could not use the token. It had been out of service for years. The kids paid with their plastic Metrocards.

The bus took them right by the cool Apple Store at 59th Street and Fifth Avenue, and since they were early, Sebastian wanted to go in and look at the iMac. Look and wish was all he could do. Sebastian knew his mother had a limited budget and there was not enough money for a fancy new computer.

Lilly and Sebastian walked down Fifth toward the dentist's office building.

Midtown in New York City was very different than the residential neighborhood where they lived. In their neighborhood, mothers wearing casual jeans or exercise tights and running shoes pushed babies in strollers. Children and teenagers walked to and from the many grammar and high schools. Old men with old hats sat on the benches on Broadway and talked and argued about something all day long. Women bent over with age pushed shopping carts on the way to and from the many food stores. There were always people walking, but the sidewalks were rarely crowded.

In midtown the sidewalks were so jammed that Lilly and Sebastian constantly had to move left or right not to bump into people coming in the opposite direction. Some of their friends' parents who wore suits and nice dresses and carried briefcases had jobs in the skyscrapers here, and they always walked like they were in a race.

Tourists from all over the world came here to experience the whole loud, bustling, taxi-honking city, to visit Rockefeller Center, and to window shop at the famous jewelry stores and designer clothing boutiques on Madison and Fifth Avenues.

Mothers with fancier haircuts and clothes than Jean ever wore shopped with their daughters. And some teenage girls not any older than Lilly shopped without their parents. They had their own credit cards to buy the clothes that filled the large shopping bags with names of expensive department stores and boutiques on them. It was as if these people had been born with their own tokens. Fifth Avenue was not the place to find someone who needed to get stronger or smarter.

Lilly and Sebastian got their teeth cleaned and the dentist did check-ups. No cavities!

On their way home, they walked through Rockefeller Center to look at the skaters on the ice rink, then took the uptown subway.

Lilly learned how to ride the trains by going on errands and explorations around the city with her mother and by studying the subway map that showed all the different train lines, each of which had a different letter or number. Today, they hopped on the Number 1 at the 49th Street and Broadway station. Luckily, they both found seats in the crowded subway car.

Lilly's responsibility to find a worthy person to pass the token to changed the way she looked at the world around her. Instead of dwelling on her own inner thoughts or worries, she looked outward.

Her mother used to say that a subway car was like a miniature New York City, a great mix of people from just about every country in the world, some with enough money in their pockets, some with too much, and some without enough.

On this train Lilly saw African Americans, Hispanics, Asians, people from India or Pakistan, and a man with red hair like her friend Seamus from Ireland. Many of them read newspapers in languages Lilly did not recognize.

There was a man and a woman studying an open map who must have been visiting from a foreign country where they didn't speak English. Next to them a young blond woman—whom Lilly thought was so pretty that she could be a model or a TV star—silently rehearsed lines from a script opened on her lap. A man who had not shaved ate some kind of food out of a container. Two young men in suits carrying briefcases worried aloud about some important appointment they were late for.

All the city school classes had ended for the day, and there were many students in the subway car heading home. They stood in small groups, talking loudly, laughing, kidding each other. Many had their phones in their hands and checked them every few moments.

Whom should she choose? The girl who never smiled? Lilly thought the girl might be sad all the time until she spoke. Her teeth were covered with complicated braces she obviously was embarrassed to show even her friends. Lilly knew that when she got the braces taken off, the girl would have a great smile.

How about the shy boy not any older than her brother who sat by himself holding a bunch of the flowers Lilly was named for? Or the heavy girl with so much eye liner and shadow she looked like a raccoon? Would the token help her stop hiding behind the makeup?

Before she had answers to these questions the train pulled into the 86th Street station and she and Sebastian got off.

On their way to their building, they walked by a church where a homeless person set up camp on the entrance steps.

They could not tell if it was a man or woman. The person wore layers of tattered overcoats. A thick winter cap was pulled low over long stringy hair. The supermarket shopping cart next to the person was filled with trash bags overflowing with used clothes. Propped up in the middle was a child's doll in a bright pink dress.

"A homeless person," Sebastian said. "Mom says they really need help."

Lilly wasn't sure she wanted to entrust the token to a homeless person because he or she might not gain strength or intelligence with it. Then she hated herself for her feeling that this person was beyond hope, so she went closer.

"Hi," Lilly said.

The pile over overcoats moved and Lilly saw it was a woman. She sat up surprisingly quickly. She held a stone in one hand, poised to use as a weapon if anyone tried to harm her or steal her junk. Her eyes were black as midnight and fierce. She spat out a torrent of curses so disgusting and angry that Lilly and Sebastian ran away. They slowed to a walk after several blocks.

"She didn't look that mean or crazy," Sebastian panted. He was a little out of breath from running.

Lilly held the token in her hand. "I can't just give this to a stranger who looks like they need it," she said.

She realized Sebastian's binoculars were useless. They could show you only what was on the surface. She thought about Monica. On the outside, she was pretty. She dressed well. She was polite, most of the time. But underneath, she was cruel.

What Lilly wanted to do was look inside. She wanted to find out what weakness needed strengthening, what fears needed to be overcome with just a little bit more courage, what lack of intelligence kept someone from becoming a better person, or what dream went unfulfilled.

She didn't have a magical x-ray machine. What she did have was family and friends and friends of friends whom she knew well enough and cared enough about to know their stories, to know what was in their hearts.

None of her relatives lived in New York or the surrounding area, and getting them the token would be a problem. So Lilly made a list of friends and friends of friends. She knew they had wishes they were unable to make happen.

Since Tommy's father had been sent overseas by the military, his mother could not control him. He hung out with the kids on the street who skateboarded in the park and smoked cigarettes and maybe took drugs. He used to be a good student. If he had the token, he would have the intelligence to see that the path he was on was leading nowhere but trouble.

Rebecca wanted more than anything to get into the special high school for the performing arts to become an actress. When she was in a tense situation, she stuttered badly, and she was terrified she would fail the audition to get into the school. The more worried she got, the worse her stuttering became. Would the token help?

Skinny David was unable to do even one chin-up in gym class, and he got teased about it all the time. The token would help him find the strength to do at least one chin-up, maybe a lot more.

But Lilly could not make the final choice.

Maybe it was because she had a nagging feeling that there was something she needed the token to find. It was mysterious to her, like trying to remember the details that would illuminate the meaning of her dream about the four people dancing or having fun in a small, crowded space.

CHAPTER 22

Late at night, after Lilly finished her homework, she sat on the window ledge in her bedroom and looked out. Lucky came over and put his head on her lap. With one hand she petted the dog, and with the other she rubbed her thumb and forefinger together on the token.

Sebastian put a new electric part into his computer and pushed the on button. Nothing happened. "Oh, man," he said. "What a dumb idea to build my own."

He saw that Lilly was lost in a thought, or a dream, like she was looking inside more than at the real world outside the window. "What are you dreaming?"

She blinked her eyes as if she had just been awoken. "Nothing really." She had been thinking about her dream. It just would not go away.

She slid off the window ledge and climbed to her bunk. Sebastian got into his bed, and Lucky hopped on, curling up near his feet. As soon as Sebastian's head hit the pillow, he was asleep. Lilly thought that maybe he could go to sleep so fast because he was eager to see what came to him in his dreams. Lilly turned out her reading light. She didn't go right to sleep, and her thoughts wandered.

She was just about to doze off when she heard Lucky whimpering. She looked down and saw he had jumped off Sebastian's bed and now stood at the window. He whined like he wanted something.

"Lucky, shhhh," Lilly whispered. "Do you need to go out, boy?"

The dog whined again, and again she shushed him.

Lucky left their bedroom and returned with her father's chewed-up red sneaker.

"Is it him?" she whispered to the dog. She climbed down to look out the window. It never really got dark in the city because of the bright streetlamps and lights glowing in the apartments. She heard footsteps approaching. "No," she said softly to herself. "It can't be Dad. Don't be such a silly boy, Lucky."

But she had hope. She didn't know where it came from or why she had it now and not before, but there it was. The footsteps came closer. They were fast and strong. Her father always walked like he was going somewhere important.

Lilly stuck her head out the window. A tall man approached in the shadows, and then he strode into the pool of light under the nearby streetlamp. It wasn't her father.

But Lucky still whimpered. What was he sensing?

Lilly thought for a long while. "Goodspeed," she said to herself. Everything worthwhile is a journey, she thought, and maybe the real journey she had been on wasn't to win a computer at the science fair. Maybe all along, even though she hadn't realized it, her journey was to find her father. She would never find him by just sitting here and dreaming and waiting. Did she have to go to California?

Lilly got the idea that Lucky was telling her that Dad was close by. How could the dog know?

She got his leash and told her mom that Lucky needed to go out to pee.

While the dog actually peed at the curb, Lilly looked around. Cars were parked close together on both sides of the street. A man sat in one of them right across from her building. Just sitting, with the car motor running.

That made Lilly uneasy. What was he doing there alone at this time of night? Creepy. She pulled Lucky in the opposite direction, but the dog wanted to go toward the car. That is when Lilly saw that the license plate was different from the New York state license plates on the other cars. She had very sharp eyesight, and even in the dim light, she could read CALIFORNIA.

Could it be him? The man's face was in shadow so she could not see clearly. All her instinct about danger in the city screamed inside her head to stay away, but she had to know. She crossed the street to walk by the car so she could see inside.

As she got close, the man turned toward her. It was her father!

"Dad?"

He powered down the passenger side window. "Hey, Lilly," he said. It was the first time she had heard his voice in over a year.

"What are you doing sitting out here in the dark?" Lilly asked.

"Trying to find some courage."

"For what?"

"To ring the doorbell."

She gave him a curious look. A fireman running into a burning building to rescue a child needed courage. She thought you did not need to be brave to ring a doorbell.

"I was afraid that you and Seb and your mom were so angry at me, you wouldn't let me in. You'd open the door and see it was me and slam it in my face."

He got out of the car and came around to her on the sidewalk. Lucky wagged his tail and licked Arthur Kemp's hand.

"You got so tall. You must be as tall as your mother now," he said.

"Just about."

"I want to come home, Lilly. Can I give you a hug?"

She didn't answer him with words, but nodded OK. He hugged her for a long moment. She didn't give him much of a hug back.

"I was afraid I lost you and Sebastian and your mom when I went away."

"You found me," she said. She hit him on the shoulder like she had done to Sebastian, but nowhere near as gently. She was glad he was back, but still a little angry he had left.

Sebastian had no mixed feelings about his father's return. When he awoke and saw his dad in the apartment, he hugged him and held his hand and leaned up against him.

Jean, however, was not all hugs and kisses. Her husband had left her and the kids almost a year ago, and he had very little communication by phone or e-mail with them or her while he was away. Being a single parent with no grandparents around to help out was tiring and often lonely. It was going to take a lot more time before she was would even consider throwing her arms around her husband.

CHAPTER 23

A rthur Kemp poured pancake batter onto a hot griddle.

Sebastian stood on a stool to be tall enough to help turn the pancake with a spatula. Lilly watched from the dining room table. Jean sat next to her reading the newspaper, more like pretending to read. She kept glancing up to see how her husband and her kids were getting along.

Sebastian pointed to the blob of batter on the griddle. "What's that?"

"It's a bunny," Arthur said. Before he went to California, he prepared breakfast for the family every Saturday morning, and his specialty was pancakes in the shapes of animals.

"A bunny? That poor bunny got run over by a car. It's a mess," Sebastian said.

"Maybe he's a little out of practice," Jean offered.

"It's a bunny," Arthur protested. "See the ears?"

Lilly got the squished bunny pancake and Arthur made a squirrel for Sebastian. But that one was just a blob too.

"Roadkill, Dad," Sebastian said. He poured syrup on it and took a bite. "But tasty roadkill."

Arthur made regular round ones for himself. Jean never liked pancakes, and she ate half a grapefruit.

They ate in silence for a moment until Arthur asked Lilly about her science fair project. From newspapers and online information websites, he collected many of the articles and photos about her and her famous centipede. He got a large envelope of clippings from his briefcase and presented it to her. She could tell he was very proud of her.

"You know I came in second in the school science fair," she said.

"But you have a new computer. I saw it in your room," Arthur said.

"One of the judges at the fair thought I should have won. So he gave it to me. I think it was just an excuse so he could ask Mom out on a date."

"Your mother is a very attractive woman," he said and smiled at Jean, who didn't really smile back. "Like mother, like daughter," he said to Lilly.

But Lilly did smile. "The guy rode up here from SoHo on his bike like it was some kind of world record for distance. He boasted how he started his own business and how dumb everyone else was compared to him and how much money he made."

"Checkmate thought he was obnoxious so he peed on him," Sebastian said.

"Smart squirrel," Arthur said.

Lilly saw he was about to ask her another question but she didn't want to talk just about herself. "Dad, did you know Sebastian is building his own computer?"

"I saw all the parts on your desk," Arthur said.

"Yeah," said Sebastian. "But the darn thing won't work."

"Let's have a look after breakfast," Arthur said.

They finished eating and washed the dishes as a team. Sebastian scraped remaining food off the plates into the garbage and handed them to Lilly, who washed them and handed them to her dad, who dried and then handed them to Jean, who put them away. The kitchen was tiny so no one could move without bumping or rubbing against the person next to them.

Now the dream came back to Lilly. The blurred faces of the four people in a cramped room came into sharp focus, and she realized she had dreamed of this moment when the family was reunited.

For reasons unknown to her, she had not dreamed about joyous family vacations where they hiked and swam in the crystal-clear lake water in the Adirondack Mountains or of Christmases at her grandparents who lived next to the world's greatest snow-sledding hill or about family picnics in Central Park.

Her dream was about doing chores together in their cramped kitchen, and that made her smile.

"What are you so happy about?" Jean asked.

"We're doing the dishes," Lilly answered. "Together."

After breakfast Arthur and Sebastian worked on building the computer.

Lilly saw them side by side at his desk, and for a moment she felt that her dad had never left. When asked, her mother told people that Arthur went to California for a job. Lilly knew that much was true.

But she was pretty sure there was more that her mother was not telling her. Was it something she or Sebastian had done to drive him away? If the reason was about her and her brother, she was sure neither her mother nor her father would tell her the truth to protect their feelings.

Maybe her parents had an argument or disagreement they could not resolve. Maybe they stopped liking each other. That happened to her friend Rachel's parents who got divorced, even though Rachel said they still loved each other, which Lilly didn't really understand. She had sometimes wondered if her father went on dates with another woman in California.

Lilly might never know the true answer. As long as her father stayed, she told herself not to wonder why he had left.

Arthur studied what his son had already assembled, then he looked over the stuff piled on the desk.

"These parts are from many different computer makers, Seb. Where did you get them?" Arthur asked.

"I find computers that people have thrown away — sometimes on the street, sometimes at school — and I take the parts I need. Mitch, the actor with the big hats next door, he gets parts for me. He calls it scrounging."

"Often parts from one kind of computer don't work with parts from another company."

"I'm finding that out."

"Try taking out that motherboard and replacing it with the other one on your desk."

They unscrewed the board and inserted the other one, then plugged in the connecting cables. Sebastian hit the on-off button. Nothing happened. He gave his father a sideways glance. That didn't work.

Arthur smiled and plugged the power cord into the wall socket. The machine did not have any electricity. "Now try it," he suggested.

Sebastian pressed the button. He heard the machine come to life. The monitor flickered, and with lightning speed the logo of a computer operating system software company appeared.

"Wow!" Sebastian yelled excitedly. He turned and slapped a high five with his father.

"All you need is a mouse and you've got yourself a really cool computer," Arthur said.

Sebastian plunged his hand into the pile of parts and, wearing a triumphant smile, pulled out a computer mouse.

While Sebastian and her father tinkered with the computer, Lilly sorted through the newspaper clippings and photos he saved for her. She tacked a photo of her mother, Dr. Hoffman, her brother, and herself onto the corkboard next to the drawing Norma made for her.

She stared at the portrait of herself. Was that what she would look like when she was grown-up? Norma had made her prettier than Lilly thought she was. And although Lilly's hair was brown, there was a rust-color tint to it in the portrait. Did Norma put a little of herself into the picture of Lilly? Were they somehow the same, like sisters?

Lilly closed her eyes and remembered the drawings in Norma's sketchbook. The ones on the left pages were filled with pain and fear and the horror of being tied up and chained. Yet on the right, the pictures of the girl dancing and moving joyfully were bursting with light.

Lilly believed the pictures were a window into Norma's true self, into her heart. Lilly saw right through Norma's street-tough armor, and what she found was someone who had been badly hurt but not permanently damaged. Someone who in a very dark night had been able to imagine a bright sunrise.

Lilly felt a surge of energy. She knew with absolute certainty to whom she would pass the token.

CHAPTER 24

B ut first Lilly had to find Norma, and she didn't know her last name or where she lived. All she knew was that she drew pictures in Brooklyn's Fort Greene Park.

Lilly told her mother most things, but not everything.

She and her brother were allowed to go just about everywhere in Manhattan by themselves. However, they did not have permission to travel to Brooklyn, which was one of the five boroughs that made up New York City. The only way to get there was over one of the three bridges connecting Brooklyn to the island of Manhattan or to take one of the many subway trains.

Lilly was determined to find the girl who drew the pictures and give her the token.

So when she and Sebastian left the house one Saturday, she told her mom they were going to the park. What Lilly failed to mention was that they were headed to Fort Greene Park, not nearby Central Park.

Lilly studied the subway map to find out which train to take, and she and Sebastian rode on the C for almost an hour to get to the Fort Greene neighborhood. The park was much smaller than Central Park. On this bright, warm day, it was filled with people playing tennis, jogging, walking dogs, and playing soccer on a dusty field. In the playground area, parents watched their kids swing and climb on the equipment.

Lilly and Sebastian walked around the entire park, and Lilly didn't see Norma anywhere. What chance was there that Norma would be here on the same day at the same time she and Sebastian were? And what if Norma didn't even live in this part of Brooklyn but had come to the park as they did on the subway train just one time, never to return?

The only place they hadn't looked was on the hill with the tall monument. They walked to the top where there were great views of the skyscrapers in lower Manhattan.

Sebastian noticed a girl sitting at the base of the tower and drawing in a sketchbook. "Is that her?" he asked Lilly.

It was. Lilly gave a sigh of relief they had not come on a fool's errand. She and Sebastian went over. "Hi," Lilly said.

"What you doing around here?" Norma asked. "You live in the city." That's what most people in Brooklyn, which is a huge city itself, called Manhattan.

"I have something for you," Lilly said.

"I don't want your charity."

"You drew a picture of you looking at my portrait in a museum. You don't want to *be* just a gangster or *be* just a patient like the kids in your neighborhood. You have a dream."

Norma swept her arm in an arc including all of Brooklyn and Manhattan. "There are a lot of dreams out there. See that smoke?" She pointed to an apartment building not far away where wispy white smoke ghosted upward out of a chimney. "It rises up and you think it's going to be something huge and wonderful, and then it just vanishes. That's what dreams are. Smoke in the air."

Lilly took the token from around her neck and offered it to Norma. "This will help you be strong and smart so your dream doesn't just disappear into the sky."

Norma looked at it and then at Lilly with disbelieving eyes.

"There's a story about it. Can we sit with you?" Lilly asked.

"I ain't going nowhere," Norma said, less anger in her voice.

"This is my brother, Sebastian. He's the storyteller." Sebastian said hi. So did Norma.

He told her that when Mr. Bernstein gave him the token, Sebastian triumphed over Rude Boy in a game of chess, and when he gave it to Lilly, she discovered a new species of centipede. Sebastian told Norma about the token's origin with the American soldier and the orphan during a long-ago war.

"And when it has given you the power you need," Sebastian said, "you must pass it along to someone who deserves it."

Again, Lilly offered it to Norma. "Believe."

Norma snorted a skeptical laugh.

"Do you play baseball?" Sebastian asked.

"I used to play softball," she said.

"You can't get a hit unless you swing. Derek Jeter told me that."

Norma shrugged her shoulders but took the token.

Lilly said earnestly, "Goodspeed."

CHAPTER 25

Lilly splashed through a shallow puddle on Central Park Drive West on her Rollerblades.

Her father jogged beside her, huffing and puffing. He wore one good red running sneaker. The other one was thoroughly chewed up. Lucky had on a harness like an Alaskan sled dog, and he pulled Sebastian on his scooter, Checkmate perched on Sebastian's shoulder. Jean ran comfortably beside Sebastian.

It was unseasonably mild for a November day. Above them the leaves were still brilliant shades of reds and oranges and yellows. An overnight rain had scrubbed the air clean, and the sky was a brilliant blue.

"You're out of shape, Dad," Lilly said.

"I have to start exercising again, Lilly. Tomorrow I'll race you on the six-mile road that loops around the entire park," he puffed. "If you take it easy on me."

"I might even let you win," she laughed.

They stopped near the rock Lilly used to climb near the Chess and Checkers House. From her backpack Jean brought out an old bed sheet, spread it out on the grass, and put out the picnic lunch: sandwiches, apples, plums, and her father's favorite brand of chocolate chip cookies. They were Lilly's favorite too, but her mother had refused to buy them when Arthur was away. Earlier in the day, when she and her mother went to the supermarket and Lilly put a box of the cookies in their shopping cart, Jean had not said no.

Arthur pulled a soccer ball out of his backpack and challenged Lilly and Sebastian to a game. They set up goals, and Arthur thought he would have no trouble scoring. But in the time he was away, both Lilly's and, in particular, Sebastian's skill levels had increased. The kids artfully passed the ball back and forth to keep it away from their father and scored much more than he did.

He finally and graciously conceded defeat, and they jogged back to where Jean was reading the newspaper. Her eyes were moist with tears.

"What's up?" Arthur asked with concern.

Jean smiled. "Listen to this," she said and read the article about the *New York Times* scholarship winners.

Every year the newspaper awarded full college scholarships to students from the city who'd overcome crushing adversity to get an education. One was a girl named Norma Little.

When she was four years old, Jean read, her parents locked her in a dark closet, often chaining her to a pipe. They rarely fed her, and when they did, it was scraps left over from their meals. They often did not let her go to the bathroom, and she slept in her own filth. No books. No TV. Almost no human contact for five years.

Lilly thought of the pictures of a child chained in a dark closet in Norma's sketchbook. Was Norma Little the Norma she had given the token to?

Jean continued to read aloud. A utility worker checking the gas meter in the house discovered the girl, and the parents were arrested for child abuse. Their excuse for their horrific behavior was that Norma had spilled chocolate milk on her church-going dress and they had to teach her to be clean.

When she was freed, she weighed only thirty pounds. She spent four months recovering her strength in a hospital, where she taught herself to read and do basic math. She then lived with a disabled relative who was very poor. To get money to feed herself and her relative, Norma had an after-school job in a neighborhood Hispanic grocery store, called a bodega, where they didn't care that she was under legal working age, as long as she was honest and worked hard.

In high school she had a ninety-six average and won several citywide art contests with her drawings. She had been accepted to the prestigious Rhode Island School of Design.

When Jean finished reading about the four other winners whose stories of hardship and determination were equally powerful, she wiped tears from her eyes. "God bless these kids," she said.

"Can I see the paper, Mom?" Lilly asked. She and her brother examined the photograph of the scholarship winners. There was Norma with a big smile. She proudly displayed the token hanging around her neck like it could have been a necklace with a huge diamond.

Lilly was so filled with emotion that tears came to her eyes. They were not tears of anger or sadness, but of joy. This time, she did not hate crying.

"For a girl," Sebastian said with a straight face, "you actually made an excellent choice who to give the token to."

He gave her a Lilly-love-tap on the shoulder. She returned the affection.

After lunch Jean and Arthur went for a walk. Sebastian wanted to join them, but Lilly knew her parents had to spend time together alone to make up for all the time they spent apart. She would read the novel she brought with her, and she asked Sebastian to keep her company. He didn't really understand, but he stayed with his sister.

Lilly had never read any of the Harry Potter books, but now she was enjoying the one about the sorcerer's stone. Lucky lay on his side, and Lilly lay beside him, resting her head on his stomach as she read.

Red Lightning came down from a high tree to play with Checkmate. Sebastian gathered up a handful of acorns, tossing them so Checkmate and his speedy friend could chase them and then hide them behind a tree for food in the winter.

Lilly put her book down. She was tired from the soccer match, and she might have eaten one too many chocolate chip cookies. She fell into a deep sleep.

She heard a soft voice.

"Lilly." Sebastian bent close to her. "Look." He was so excited, his voice got higher than it already was.

She saw the snow leopard on top of her climbing rock. It was scary and wonderfully beautiful at the same time. The wildest of wild animals was right in the middle of a city with eight million human beings, an environment as different from its natural habitat as it could possibly be. Behind him were not remote windswept mountains of central Asia, but concrete and steel and glass skyscrapers.

Was this a dream? If it was, it was filled with color like Sebastian's dreams and was the most realistic one she ever had.

"He got free," Lilly said to Sebastian. "He escaped from the zoo."

Then she saw it—dangling around the leopard's neck.

Lilly burst out laughing. "Norma! Norma hated seeing anyone or anything confined in a cage. She must have decided that the leopard needed to get smarter and stronger so..."

"So he could have the power to escape," Sebastian said.

Lilly motioned to the big cat to come down from the rock. The leopard leaped, and he seemed to float in slow motion, landing softly as a Kleenex dropped to the floor. He came over to Lilly and Sebastian. They both petted him and leaned against his soft fur.

Lucky and Checkmate backed off a little way.

"Don't worry, Checkmate," Lilly assured the squirrel. "He won't make a snack out of you. Don't be scared, Lucky. He won't eat you for dinner. He's a member of our pack."

As Lilly and Sebastian rubbed their hands over the leopard's soft fur, he purred. The sound was so low, the kids could feel it in their chests.

They heard police sirens getting closer and closer. "I'm sure that's the zookeepers and the park police coming after him," Lilly said.

"They might hurt him," Sebastian worried.

"Then we have to take him home," Lilly told her brother.

"Our apartment isn't very big, and I think Miss Flannigan will be scared when she hears the leopard roar."

"Not our home. His home."

"But you said that was across all of America, then over an ocean, and then across miles and miles of desert. Where will we get food? Where will we sleep? There will be no cell phones where we're going. There could be cruel pirates on the ocean and cannibals on the deserts who want cook us in a big pot of boiling water and eat us up."

"Do you not want to come?" Lilly asked.

She saw him narrow his eyes like he always did when he was thinking hard. After a long silence, he stood as tall as he could and said, "We have Lucky and the leopard to scare any bad guys away. It'll be a grand adventure."

"Yes," Lilly said. "An adventure."

She petted the leopard. "We're going to find your mountaintop."

The big cat growled. Sebastian and Lilly knew it was not a scary growl. It was a grateful, friendly growl.

Lilly hitched the rope from Lucky's harness to Sebastian's scooter. He pulled on his helmet and motioned for Checkmate to hop on his shoulder. But Checkmate wanted to stay alongside Red Lightning. The police sirens were very close now.

Lilly hopped on the leopard's back. "Let's go."

Off they went. Lucky pulled Sebastian, and the leopard ran with an easy stride. He was happy to have the freedom to really run after being inside the cage for so long. Checkmate and Red Lightning kept up, leaping from tree to tree above them.

They all headed north in the park. Lilly knew Manhattan was an island, and the only way off was through the tunnels or over one of the bridges. She was confident she could find one where they could escape into the countryside.

On a bench near the Chess and Checkers House, Mr. Bernstein read his newspapers. He looked up. What he saw was strange, but since seeing new and fantastic sights is one of the delights of living in New York City, a big smile came across his face.

The token dangling on a long chain around the snow leopard's neck glistened as the sun reflected off it. Lilly crouched low on the snow leopard's back, grasping his fur so she would not slide off. With one hand she waved to Mr. Bernstein, and he waved back.

"We're taking the leopard home, Mr. B!" Sebastian yelled.

Mr. Bernstein called back, "Goodspeed!"

THE END

Note: The *Nannarrup hoffmani* centipede was discovered several years ago, and it actually was the first new species to be found in Central Park in over one hundred years.

For their comments
and encouragement,
my deepest thanks go out to:
Betsy
Pam
Peter
Samantha
Michael
Sophia
Julia
And always,
Nina

20936179R00093

Made in the USA
Charleston, SC
31 July 2013